Henry Llewellyn Williams

The Queen of the Drama Mary Anderson

Henry Llewellyn Williams

The Queen of the Drama Mary Anderson

ISBN/EAN: 9783337376789

Printed in Europe, USA, Canada, Australia, Japan

Cover: Foto ©Andreas Hilbeck / pixelio.de

More available books at **www.hansebooks.com**

. THE

"QUEEN OF THE DRAMA!"

MARY ANDERSON:

HER LIFE ON AND OFF THE STAGE.

TOGETHER WITH

SELECT RECITATIONS

FROM ALL THE GREAT PLAYS

IN WHICH SHE HAS DELIGHTED TWO CONTINENTS.

BY HENRY L. WILLIAMS.

Translator of "The Wandering Jew," "The Hunchback of Notre Dame," "Theodora," etc.

———◆———

NEW-YORK:

PUBLISHED FOR THE TRADE.

NO. 3 NORTH WILLIAM STREET.

CONTENTS.

[iii]

iv.

LIFE OF MARY ANDERSON.

"The Advent of the Star."

On the 28th day of July, 1859, Mary Anderson was born at Sacramento, California. She was left a half orphan, by her father being killed in the Confederate States service at the destruction of the defenses of Mobile, August 5th and 6th, 1861, the child being but little over her second year.

"Old Kaintuck's" Claims.

Only six months after her birth, little Mary was taken by her mother to Louisville, where she was being brought up under maternal care. Both father and mother had some dramatic talent, and even as a tiny child, Mary showed more than the usual proclivity of the juvenile for mimicry in snatches of verse and declamation. When her mother married again, there arose no bar to this innate tendency, as her stepfather, Dr. Hamilton Griffin, ex-surgeon of the Southern army, was similarly fond of the stage.

The Budding Propensity

thus fostered, "Mimi" (as the household caressingly styled her) imbibed Shakespeare till so surcharged

that it was not sufficient relief to repeat " Richard
III." to admiring friends of the family in the "Back
Parlor Theatre " but all over the house literally; the
colored servants being often startled by fiercely thril-
ling outbursts from the same tyrant "King Dick" or
petrified by blood-curdling passages of "Hamlet."

To feed this rising flame, the girl from her tenth
year had been liberally taken to the play, and her im-
itations of entire scenes with the mannerisms of the
performers, were generally considered, making due
allowance for the ease with which the gallant Kentuc-
kian is kindled to enthusiasm by young womanhood,
to prove much retentiveness of memory and ability
to reiterate in clearness and fidelity. A good ear for
music accompanied these gifts, and enhanced the ac-
curacy of the repetition, where the piece had been mel-
odramatic.

In the midst of these gropings, not assisted by any
one of *professional* experience, the round of characters played by Edwin Booth at the Louisville theatre
witched the girl and directed her inclination to the intellectual school of acting as contradistinguished from
the muscular division of Forrest and McCullough.
Edwin Booth remains her ideal of Roscius, and she
still believes him unequalled in the Shakespearian
walk.

He was then no longer the youth who delighted, at
the Winter Garden, the first worthies of New York ;
but he had worn away much of the peculiarities of his
father and his father's type whom Edmund Kean had
eclipsed just as they had the Kemble tribe. He was,
therefore, a glass of fashion which the aspirant had
fortunately set before her.

She returned home, particularly fired in fancy by Booth's melancholy Dane, and with a determination to figure upon the boards where such an ornament was becomingly enframed.

Her mother, with the Southern's pride, objected to a public exhibition of what she had commended pleasantly within closed doors, but she was prevailed upon by her husband to bow to the girl's instance.

Hence, in 1873, Miss Anderson began to study seriously for the stage under Mr. George Vandenhoff the veteran actor and well-famed teacher of elocution.

There was hardly a better professor to have been selected for a pupil intended to tread the higher plateaux of Parnassus. Not merely was this gentleman a thoroughly inured comedian and tragedian whose name is entwined with the most sunny season of the British poetic drama, but to moral grandeur he has inestimable claims. We may cite one memorable example when at the foremost comedy playhouse in London, he indignantly broke his engagement rather than approve the foisting upon the classic boards of a notorious woman, not merely unworthy but incompetent, solely because her introducer was a money-lender to the embarrassed manager. With such an instructor, there was no fear, it follows, for the scholar to entertain a mean opinion of her chosen class.

This tuition went on some two years, relieved by that in dancing and gymnastics, giving half a day to all.

In 1875, the declining glory of the American theatre, Miss Charlotte Cushman, that monument of devotion to sisterly affection, almost dying of an incurable malady, was at Cincinnati, purposing a visit for health to California's bracing climate.

Mr. Vandenhoff had played with her "long time ago," and as she had acquired a great deal of stage knowledge from his god Macready, he thought it excellent to have her opinion and counsel upon the jewel that he was polishing. Miss Cushman came to the Griffins, and after a brief interview with Miss Anderson, and hearing her recite, approved and predicted that with a continuance of this judicious training and some five years practice, she would rank among the first if not be the foremost, of her profession in the United States.

We should like a faithful picture of that momentous interview: the grave Yankee veteran, hallowed by the fadeless memory of her conquering the plaudits of stubborn England, smiling serenely with the consciousness of a deserved meed eternal for her self-sacrifice and patient sufferings—and the daughter of the Golden State, at sweet shrinking yet glowing fifteen, her auburn hair shining with the reflection of the splendid aureole which the grey-head wore.

Such was the impression upon the novice that a dream ensued: she thought that she beheld the old actress, on whom the hand of death so ostensibly lay, already dead, and on her bier, covered with the flag of the country and her well-earned laurels. As she gazed spellbound, she heard the moving voice, as the tragedienne rose from her casket, thunder, "Play 'Medea!'" But it will be many years before the slight, gentle successor of "Our Charlotte" attempts a character of that antique iron mould, and of the strict Cushman repertoire, the gipsy crone in "Guy Mannering" is the sole one she annexed and that prematurely.

The First Appearance.

Towards the close of 1875, taught, trained, fortified, Miss Vaulting Ambition, was looking about for that occasion which inevitably arrives to the properly prepared.

On a Thursday the twenty fifth of November, 1875, having come with her stepfather from their out-of-town home into Louisville, they ran up against Mr. Macauley, proprietor manager of the theatre bearing his name. He was perturbed: some "star" actress had failed to make a railroad connection (it was Miss Jane Coombs, we believe,) and yet the bills were out "for Saturday ——the playgoers of Louisville were promised "Romeo and Juliet." "All the rest are ready, to the last button of their gaiters," said Mr. Macauley, half in a moan, half in a forced jocularity, and no Juliet! Upon my word, doctor, I would give you a stage box for life—and may you attain that of Joyce Heath!——if you would lend me this young lady for Saturday!"

Appear as Juliet? that exacting character of which everybody knows it has been said that it is not possible in the nature of things since when the necessary study and experience have been obtained, the youthful charm which such a personage demands, must long have departed.

But angels rush in where even folly would have hesitated to leap, the doctor snapped at the offer, the young lady left the twain to cement the compact, and flew home to tell her mother that "it was no longer night, the dawn had come!"

On Saturday, November the twenty seventh, then, Miss Mary Anderson made her first appearance on any stage —"a young lady of this city"—at Macauley's

Theatre, Louisville, in the part of Juliet, in the borrowed costume of the stage manager's good wife. (It caught her under the arms, it is true, but the enchanted audience did not think the young genius cramped in the least!)

The Southern Tour.

Though the manager joined in the approval of this debut, the arrival of the actress engaged postponed any immediate result. However, during some weeks the press echoed the inquirer of that Saturday night's audience for the new-comer, and Mr. Macauley offered a regular engagement.

It commenced on the twentieth day of the second month of the new year. The disadvantages were many : notably that of insufficient rehearsals, only one being given to each play, and those plays were important ones, of the long five-act class: "Fazio," the "Hunchback," and their sort. Nevertheless, the success of the aspirant was encouraging, not merely by what the spectator thought, but what a business man did.

Mr. John T. Ford, of Baltimore, believed he said in Miss Anderson, "the Coming American Tragedienne," so long prophesied. He engaged her for a long Southern tour which was to afford her practice in sufficiency to enable her to confront the patrons of the Washington and Baltimore theatres. Once again, Miss Anderson was as fortunate as when Mr. Vandenhoff was her instructor, for Mr. Ford is one of those men of honor who carry out a business contract with perfect loyalty, and nothing was neglected during the circuit. (Mr. Ford is one of our few managers who make it a point to pay foreign authors even for those pieces which be-

ing first acted abroad, can in strict law have no claim
to that effect.)

It was the Centennial Year, and all the money it was
believed, was being garnered for spending at Phila-
delphia. Nevertheless, the new "star" did as well,
comparatively, in the Gulf and Atlantic States as Miss
Neilson, the English favorite, in the North.

In March, St. Louis acclaimed her first essay as
Pauline, and the following month, New Orleans was
startled by her audacity and self-abnegation in trying
to make a duly hideous Meg Merriless, in remembrance of that powerful impersonation of Charlotte
Cushman. The *N. O. Bulletin* considered the actress's
physique too slight for the hardy crone, but concluded
that the performance was still remarkable in one who
had only once seen the part (*i. e.* heard Miss Cushman
recite portions), and with the strength and experience
which come with well-spent years, Miss Anderson will
make no unworthy successor to Charlotte Cushman.

In August, she appeared in her native state, and repeated this Meg Merriless at the California Theatre,
San Francisco, together with Evadne, Bianca, and "In
gomar" for the first time, as Parthenia, since a favorite with herself and her admirers.

At the end of 1876, Miss Anderson had become an
object of interest to the theatre frequenters of cities
where she was unknown by sight. This fact was clear
that audiences liked and commended her,—whilst the
journals spoke harshly, unjustly in fact to one so
young, in novel surroundings. Why blame a mere
girl for deficiences in "make-up" when, apart from a
little rouge and powder, hardly more than fashiona-
bles wear at a ball, she had no need to beautify her-

self. Why pretend the fine, supple and commanding form owed much to a costly wardrobe, when classical costumes are surely within the power of a limited purse, and no one was ever of the opinion that the Statue Bride, the Barbarian Chieftain's Subduer, and Harry Bertram's Protectress had been garishly attired· It was said that Chicago was captious simply because the rival city of St. Louis had belauded the rising luminary, but why the Baltimore press should have been more bitter than that of Chicago or San Francisco, was inexplicable, in fair play. Out of all the criticisms —honeyed or envenomed—came this succint report of "the Great Western Prodigy:" a girl of seventeen, five feet seven and a half in height, 140 lbs. weight, (these details would have been more suitable in "the nation of shopkeepers," we think) naturally talented. with a fine contralto voice.

In 1877, the possessor of these gifts ventured to present herself as Lady Macbeth, at the National Theatre, Washington. She was not framed to offer the Scandinavian helpmate of the warrior, who rather hectored him into crime than cajoled him. But it was after the Mrs. Siddons' vein, a seductive creature who tempts her husband to seize the crown with a murderer's reeking hand in order to have her children royal. But Miss Anderson was too young to embody the popular ideal, be it one or the other type, and it was such a shortcoming as Miss Kate Bateman provided in her youth when her appearance, slight, fair, girlish, in the scene to read her husband's letter from the camp, naturally suggested that Lady Macbeth had deputed her eldest daughter to apologize for her!

About this time an *Acrostic* was addressed to the young actress, which we here append. It is chiefly notable because the writer already seemed to have divined the classical possibilities of the future *Galatea* realizing the ideas in form and feature of the Atheman and Corinthian sculptors.

It must be remembered that at this time, Miss Anderson had never gazed upon the original of "that statue that enchants the world" nor on those other faultless marbles which seem to have leaped out of the quarry, perfect in all the attributes of loveliness, rather than to have been deftly carved by the inspired artist.

That we have not sought "to paint the lily" will appear from this opinion of a famous French writer: "This lady's face is divinely fair and gentle, the expression candid and fearless, the grace indescribable and the profile classic. Gerard would not have wanted ed a more graceful or chaster model to paint Psyche receiving the first kiss of love."

To Mary Anderson.

M aid at whose birth the Olympian Muses Nine
A ttended with their various gifts divine.
R ight royally endowing thee that hour,
Y oung Genius, with each Goddess' special power.

A perfect form!—Canova's marble grace!
N o hand save Raphael's ere could paint thy face!
D uctile as wax, to show in every part,
E ach niching Passion of the human heart—
R evenge, Pride, Jealousy, Remorse and Love,
S uch as in all great Shakespeares heroine's move,
O n thy charmed head Heaven's choicest blessings light,
N or one cloud lower thy happiness to blight.

                                        H. L. W.

1878 revealed improvement and testified that the modesty which had been hastily condemned as coldness was approved by the intellectual and refined classes, who again trooped to the theatre, no longer desecrated by flimsy spectacular farces, French singsongs and caucans, and heavy adaptations from the still heavier German *originals*, themselves clumsy translations of Parisian comedies.

After another Southern tour, to reward her firstmade friends with a view of her justifying their old welcome, the promising actress went to Europe (June to September,) chiefly to replenish a wardrobe which would not place "the Hope of the Native Stage" below the Rousbys and Nielsons in respect to dress and jewels: in other respects, she was fully equipped.

A letter to Madame Bernhardt was the key to all Parisian theatre doors, and this "pale shadow of Rachel" received her young sister in art quite cordially.

As for Madame Ristori, a lady in all the unbounded meaning of the word, she has a sincere love for America, and *la Signorina Columbia* was most affectionately dealt with.

There was no one on the English stage entitled to rank with the great: Miss Ellen Terry is a reflex of her elder sister Kate who, herself, at her acme, was often "played down" by her "understudy," Miss Lydia Foote; Mrs. Kendal ("Tom" Robertson's sister) is merely a great emotional comedian, inferior to Miss Clara Morris for power. Among the old stagers, Mr. Mead, Mr. Ryder, and Mrs. Stirling remain, irreplaceable.

In fact, no one to copy, none to emulate, none to fear as rivals.

Not to form a resolve to seize this unoccupied fane would have been incompatible with the daring temperament of an American.

She returned home, still one of the youngest and about the most conspicuous star.

In these few years, crudities had been brushed off, she had gained "repose," and rather too much of the evenness which sensational actors, like Lemaitre, had denounced as inferior to the slurring intervals in order to capture with "points"

The universal "they" began to contrast her with Madame Modjeska.

Her popularity and drawing power were shown to to be increased; in collegiate towns, students showed their "drawing power," by the way, in severing the traces of her carriage horses, and transporting her from stagedoor to hotel, as their substitutes.

The Northern and Eastern cities beheld her in now familiar rôles and as Bertha ("Daughter of Roland," a life-lacking translation from the wordy modern French,) and Julia (first time in New York, 5th Sept. 1878.) Still unequal, too often forgetting the individuality of the part, there yet arose evidence of that seeking to improve which the appreciative play goer values as much as perfection itself, for it irritates his attention into perpetual activity. There had been an absurd calumny that the praises of the foreign dramatic eminences had turned "Our Mary's" head, but she has the true sense of the born actress and as Macready used to say "crowded houses or with only two in the pit, let us not put on any airs."

The New Y k press, laying aside gushing "as out of place, tre . . .t the performances in a tone grateful to the recipient and pointed out little defects purely for correction in order the most promising standard-bearer of American Art should be absolutely faultless when carrying the flag to conquer new worlds.

This just and seemly tone was eminently due to the exertions of Mr. Sylvester M. Hickey and Mr. Pomeroy, whose firm yet fervid writings upon the tragedienne soon counterpoised and eventually overbalanced the extravagancies of the Out-Western papers which formerly prejudiced the Atlantic cities against the subject of such strained eulogy.

Galatea in the Gilbertian play "Pygmalion and Galatea" was added to the growing repertoire by 1882, during the summer of which year Miss Anderson, in her villa near Long Branch, meditated on "the Conquest of England."

The Actress at Home.

The theatrical colony at the watering-place of Long Branch is unique. The European players who are recommended quiet are compelled to go far afield. On the contrary, the little *rus in urbe* of the American theatrical world is exclusive and, within it pale undisturbed rest is really obtainable. The principal managers and actors have villas ; that of Miss Anderson is a handsome house, altered after her own design, in Cedar Avenue. Shunning even the appearance of seeking notoriety, the novelist who chose her for a heroine could hardly say she "might be seen" on the spacious lawn with her handsome mother, her little half-sister, her brother (who acts with her in small parts,) and her

deerhound Uno. But a glimpse may be 1   hen she
rides out with her stepfather or brother F. nk, who
has become an actor, or cruises in her steamer the
doubly appropriately named "Galatea." Within doors
she follows Longfellow's advice that the high-type actress should see a beautiful picture (that's herself in
the morning mirror! saith our pen involuntarily, probably of gallant Limerick steel,) read a beautiful book
(she tempers the classics with Dickens,) and her beautiful music (she sings to herself not unseldom.) Around
her are theatrical mementoes, furniture from sales of
dramatic queens of England, portraits and busts of her
earliest idol, Edwin Booth, and of her latest, Henry
Irving—quite refined, you see in taste. Here the
"cold and classical "one unbends, aye, enjoys a humor-
ous story, and even smokes a cigarette. Alas! the or-
namental cattle are sold off, weeds throttle the roses,
and their seems some foundation for the rumor that,
after our farewell round of performances, Miss Anderson will take a theatre in London.

On the Eve of the Plunge.

To prevent North America tilting up by the pre-
ponderance of so much talent on the eastern board as
that of Mr. Irving and Miss Anderson, Mr. Abbey determined to execute an exchange of the two articles
from their own to the confronting countries. In Mr.
Irving's London Lyceum Theatre, from Sept. 1st to
June 1st, 1883, the acknowledged representative of our
stage was to test the discrimination rather than the
kindness of the British public.

These were her credentials not as we might patri-
otically state them, but in the words of Mr. Moy

Thomas, the London *Daily News* dramatic critic:
"Figure, slight but not spare; features, regular but
full of expression; pose of the small head, graceful;
manner girlishly pretty; method, extremely winning;
bearing, singularly refined; voice, melodious; accent
(that terrible American accent which is, usually a per-
sonal peculiarity and not national at all!) slight and
seldom unpleasing."

Add, or, rather, place above all, unsullied reputation.
Not one of her well-earned dollars has gone to hush a
scandal or to advertise one that would allure an audi-
tor of the badder sort; and no lady ever blushed to
learn that the actress whom she had praised was the
heroine of some abominable incidents in real life.   When
Miss Anderson sailed from New York for Liverpool,
May the twenty-ninth, 1883, she was the pure, perfect
chrysolite of the American Drama.

"Parthenia" in London.

Except that fifty thousand photographs of Miss Anderson had been sold in England, and this plainly to
gratify the æsthetic, nothing whatever had been done
in laying a train for an explosion.   The result probably
justifies her enterprises, but how unlike the usual mode
by which "stars" have gained borrowed lustre! what,
no "extra" charged columns of encomiums in the
theatrical and daily papers! no inspired trumpettings
the clippings from the American papers which were
reprinted owing to their extravagance or that "wild
western wit" which is Chaldee to the Londoner.   And
then in the interval before the ordeal, Miss Anderson's
residence in St. John's Wood received not one of the
wiseacres who meant to initiate "the griffin" "into

our ways "—on the contrary the lady was determined to preserve her American individuality." As for those dramatic critics who were also dramatic authors, and who "fished" to learn if some manuscript in their dus-tiest portfolio was not preferable to that musty and dreary old "Ingomar," they never crossed the thresh-old. The consequent wrath in the literary and Bohe-mian clubs was palpable, and all these experts in sneer-ing prepared beforehand those articles which oftener show off the ability of the writer than that of the victim discussed. As before said, however, there was not one single actress able to vie with the American, in many points, especially in youth and comeliness.

One lady alone was understood to fear her the most, for Miss Anderson had thrown down the gauntlet to her in the announcement to play a part of which she was the original expositor. This little item in the programme had irritated all St. James' like an ele-phant-fly the ponderous yet sensitive pachederm.

The critics had predoomed the stranger, we say, from the moment when her characters were found to be obselete ones which *they* had never seen unless in their boyhood. This fact alone evinces how they had "lost touch" with the people. "Fazio," "the Hunch-back," "the Lady of Lyons," and the like, thanks to running out of copyright, were only recently emanci-pated from excessive charges, so that now the innu-merable amateur societies and playbook readers could become familiar with them. As a consequence, fifty thousand young people were eager to see them played and the pivot-rôle made visible and sympathetically sentient. And the young artists who had devoured Miss Anderson's portraits were as wistful as that band of first-nighters, ravenous liegemen of the drama, who scored the first Saturday in December as a sight not to be missed. Moreover, Mr. Irving had besought in his farewell speech before departure to America, "the heartiest English welcome to the lady whose beauty and talent had made her a favorite from California to Maine," and the Irvingites were in fidelity bound to muster in force. Think, too, of "the American colony," gratified with American this and American that throughout the center of civilization : Edison lights on the Viaduct, Westinghouse brakes to the Pullman cars on all rails running to the great city, Reinhart's drawings centrally in the *Graphic's* window; American salmon on the breakfast table, American beef bringinga ,better price than the home-grown, American biscuits at tea, and American preserves topping dinner!

Altogether, truly, a very remarkable audience in the temple of to-day's dramatic favorite of fortune.

It may be interesting to analyze this very remarkable audience : of the gallery and pit components mention has been made—in the boxes and stalls were noblemen, officers of the Queen's body guard, Members of Parliament, law and even clerical magnates—although to all these the attractions of moor and mountain and ocean were forgone), authors, critics, Miss Kate Terry, half out of her box to gesticulate to friends, Horace Lingard, P. T. Barnum, (fresh from another inspection of the Crystal Palace, counterpart of the Alexandra, sighing to embrace the e-nor-mous World's Show), Bronson Howard (with the disposition in London of " Young Mrs. Winthrop " on the brain), Miss Emily Faithful, Miss Braddon, Joseph Hatton,

James Mortimer, (the Franco-American Journalist who has not quite yet won London to stomach a "live" journal,) the veteran tragedian Creswick, Genevieve Ward, Mrs. Raymond (recovered from Roman fever and looking as beautiful as that Dusseldorf portrait of hers inseparable as Fanny Bombance's in "Tricoche"), Farjeon (as Australia's representative,) Lord Garmoyle and Miss Fortescue in a "celebrated case," and over all the countless bouquets' odor, that of the immense basket of lilies to be offered from the Jersey Lily to the Magnolia.

When this vast audience had quieted down from a babble as unprecedently noisy as that of a New Orleans carnival ball when the music suddenly pauses, all was expectation for the heroine of the "as bad a play as was ever written" (*Truth.*)

Miss Anderson's reception was tremendous. The first impression was delightful (*Referee.*) "No criticism (said Mr. Sala in the *Illustrated London News*) will bar the fact that there is no more beautiful woman on the stage, she is fully as highly favored as Mr. Rousby, but carries herself with greater dignity, and her movements are more symmetrical." *Society* asserted that "only classical times had got so classical a face," though adding its wonder that "in the youngest of nations the old type should be revived."

Mr. Sala said the voice was singularly rich, melodious, powerful, flexible and resonant, the voice of tragedy, whilst the *Referee*, more particular states: "The voice, has at moments a strong accent, sounded strange at first to our English ears, and in the earlier scenes the actress had not caught the pitch of the theatre, and spoke too low— a fault brought into notice in a

not unkindly fashion by an outspoken critic in the top
gallery, whose suggestion she instantly adopted. There
is a kind of music in it all the same, and the tendency
to over-accentuate the "r's," and over-emphasise the
first syllable of such words as "pro-file" and Par-thenia"
can be easily conquered."

The criticisms are full of interest, and the ones of
importance are appended: *Era* (the organ of theatri-
cals, nicknamed therefore "the Actors' Bible"):—It
was "a gratifying success" of "a great actress come
among us" and "a more beautiful or more perfect impersonation of Parthenia it is not possible to conceive."

Athæneum (the leading literary organ):—"An excellent and ideal interpretation of Parthenia by an actress of intellect and mark, with a method incomplete
as yet but of distinct value."

Academy:—"Miss Anderson, a new and potent
stage attraction, has conquered and fascinated, and a
success won in such a dull piece as "Ingomar" may
count for almost as much as a triumph won elsewhere.
It is an agreeable foretaste of what this delightful actress may accomplish in a character more obviously
worthy than grace above beauty."

Vanity Fair (the chief aristocratic organ):—"Although icily faultless, there are possibilities of passion in her not yet given utterance to."

Whitehall Review:—"The unqualified success of a
true artist."

The World (Edmund Yates' paper):—"Quite the
most complete and charming actress America has ever
given England (and yet Mr. Yates may have seen Mrs.
Anna Cora Mowatt)—a mistress of her art. In graceful motion many an English artiste might learn a lesson in deportment with advantage."

Truth (Mr. Labouchère's paper): — "In her love scenes her comedy is unforced and her sentiment has none of that wearisome gush with which we are so often bored, whilst on the few occasions to display force it was manifested without effort, exaggeration or rant."

Queen (the fashionable ladies' journal):—" The most finished and accomplished actress the transatlantic stage has submitted to our judgment; totally free from affectation."

Baily's Magazine (circulating among the nobility and richer gentry):—"A more delightful Parthenia has never been seen. It is no small proof of talent that she changed Ingomar into the 'second fiddle.' The cold and indifferent audience of the first scene, became warmly enthusiastic in the second, till she conquered us as well as the rough barbarian."

Society:—"Nothing short of genius could surely overcome, in an era conspicuous for cynicism and irreverence, in an old-fashioned, ultra romantic play, remarkable for stilted diction and sentimental situations. The amount of comedy infused was quite, unusual and contributed in no small measure to complete success."

Graphic (artistic):—"Altogether entitled her to a place in the foremost rank of our English actresses."

Illustrated London News (G. A. Sala):—"An actress of the very highest capacity, but as yet I fail to discern genius in her acting."

Morning Post (known as "Jeames," after Thackeray's footman, from being *the* chronicler of the upper class's movements and opinions):—"Not genius, but talent; beautiful, winsome, gifted, accomplished."

Daily News: (Moy Thomas, critic): "Altogether

Miss Anderson has every grounds of satisfaction with her present surroundings."

Pall Mall Gazette:—"A brilliant success of a dangerous and difficult experiment. The triumph of the actress involves the vindication of a play long held up to ridicule as a specimen of fustian. The whole is well thought out, is perfect in beauty, and rises at parts into intensity all but tragic, of admirably played scenes."

Standard (conservative) : — "A complete success. A real power of delineating passion was exhibited and in the scene where *Parthenia* repulses the advances of her too venturesome admirer and in this direction, to our mind, the best efforts of the lady tend. As in the case of Salvini, in fact with any actor of the highest rank, there is always a reserve of power."

Sunday Times: — "Intensely *sympathique,* she did not disappoint expectation, and she has almost without an effort already made her mark on the English stage, and received a welcome not only deserved, but worthy of those who speak a common language and have so many tastes and sympathies in common."

Referee : — "She came, was seen, and conquered."

We give the above in profusion, for it must be gratifying to perceive that we were not deluded into unfounded eulogy of our fellow-countrywoman.

The story of this memorable night is that her appearance was the signal for a tremendous outburst of applause which almost unnerved her, for she is always a victim of stage fright. (So much so that, at her first essay of boys parts in "Ion," like that of Madame Nilsson at Cherubino, her limbs smote one another with tremor, and the transient impression was that she was not strong!) the first scene went by in oppressive silence, for the audience was studying for an opinion. In the third act, grace and tenderness lighted up by genuine flashes of power elicted an outburst of spontaneous applause which rose far above mere demonstrations of friendliness, and her position was established. In the episode where Parthenia assumes the helm and takes the spear, striking the attitude of Pallas, Bellona, Venus with the weapons of Mars, or any other classical image that corresponds, the resemblance to *La Bell* Stewart as Britannia on the current coin caused the gods and pitites to deem it a compliment to the British Lion, and he roared with all his might and *main*.

It is to be clearly understood that most of this eulogy was wrung from the critics. In private, they carped, all the more fretfully, as spite of their undermining, the people of all classes, many not usually attenders to histrionic sights, gravitated as by the instinct of a diamond finder, to the Lyceum.

Miss Anderson was becoming the rage and the endless file of carriages at the Lyceum galled the hostile "newspaper-men" as they went along to Printinghouse Avenue. "It is equally certain that she owes this position in a very slight degree to published accounts of her acting," confessed a paper of the 15th Dec., 1883. "From the first she has been received, with only a few exceptions, only in a coldly critical spirit; and yet her reputation has gone on gathering in strength till the house is crowded nightly. There is no possible explanation except that her acting affords pleasure in a high degree." The solid test, the solid fact that the new attraction drew more money in a given time than ever before was drawn to Mr. Irving's theatre (*Referee*). The agitation was increased when a change of the bill to "the Lady of Lyons" was announced.

Her Second Character.

Though some of the detractors were resolved to remain unconverted by Miss Anderson's "Pauline" it brought over several from the enemy's camp. It is true Lord Lytton's perennial play was abused as uninteresting (*World*), superficial in sentiment and tricky in poesy (*Daily Telegraph*), of which every playgoer is well tired (*Bailey's Magazine*); nevertheless, it always fills a house with reasonably competent performers, and in truth "the very backbone" monetarily of the English Dramatic Authors' Society, for which we have the manager, playright, and actor Henry J. Byron's word. Hence the irritation of spouting dramatists at Alcibiades Bulwer persisting in never-dying.

Miss Cavendish was too unfeeling, Miss Ellen Terry too weak as Pauline, and there was a confident foreboding that the new one would eclipse them all in the proud and romantic belle of Lyons.

Prominent in the assemblage, as numerous and brilliant as ever was seen, of all noble, lovely, artistic and literary London, Lady Burdett-Coutts was visible, the head of charitable wealth, and the Princess of Wales (whose immaculate reputation stamps the actress whom she applauds, as one of the morally elect). The contemned old-fashioned play was listened to with breathless attention, save when tumultuous applause interrupted and the pit called as on a Kean or Siddons night for "three cheers more" at the close an event unknown to the writer's twenty years experience of the London stage and tasking the everlasting Charles Hervey's recollection itself.

The *critiques* show the stunning impression of that pronounced enthusiasm. The physical charm was granted as at the first: "In the poetry of motion, she certainly equals, perhaps surpasses any living actress (*Life*)."—"A quality of girlishness about it that makes it totally distinct from any Pauline I have seen (*Vanity Fair.*)" "It will undeniably strengthen the hold already secured on the admiration of English playgoers (*Era*)." "A captivating performance, and a newcomer has to be welcomed as an actress of high mark. She is an almost ideal representative of the tenderest Shaksperian conceptions (*Athœneum*)." "In it everything to admire. It is difficult to see how the heroine could have been more skilfully represented, and to suggest any improvement that rare and intelligent forethought could bring, or to point out any error of judgment (*Standard*)."— "A singularly fine, picturesque tender and impassioned performance. In grace and beauty, it comes scarcely if at all behind her Parthenia while it reveals the possession of a totally different range of talents. Her art is broader than was first surmised. The triumph belonged wholly to Miss Anderson—a triumph more undisputed and more honorable has seldom been chronicled" (*Pall Mall Gazette*). —"Every movement was effective from not being done for effect (*World*).

The Claude of the evening had rather threatened to shout her down, being of the robust school, but that, perhaps, had its advantage of keeping the actress's voice up to the level and proving that it was one "capable of both light and grave expression ; sarcasm and fierce scorn, full of power and serenity (*Graphic*.)

This time, the debutante could not plead nervousness. There was much amusement when a glance was given to the royal box at the line "*Princes* are *so* changeful," which elicited a smile from the wife of Albert Edward, and that exalted dame crowned the delightfully successful Pauline by sending round for the American lady to visit her in the box. As the actress never sees any one unconnected with the play during its progress, that was impossible. Since Mr. J. S. Clarke gave the Prince of Wales a lesson in the duty of all public characters towards the public, by having the Strand Theatre curtain rung up at the appointed hour, although the expected guest was leisurely arriving, never was a lofty personage so amazed. Nevertheless, the good sense of her Highness seconded her kind nature, and she dallied over her enrobing at the departure so that Miss Anderson could come round and receive her bouquet as a testimonial of her gratification. The future queen's favor is everything to the English, and during the week when the incident was reported, the newspaper writers reflected. As for her being the idol of the play going public, that might not affect them. "Critics are sometimes wrong ; the public never," is a passable maxim, but critics never acknowledge their failures, like Brummel's valet. However, something had to be done, for, already, the tone of discussion had become deeper, and the casual reader himself met such striking contradictions as "with a single flash of real emotion, Miss Anderson would be perfect." (*Queen*), "artistic but not wholly natural" (*Whitehall Review*), and "a good *actress* " (*Daily Telegraph*), contrasting with "an adept at depicting passion (*World*)," and "with the power to move deeply shown in more than one very fine outburst" (*Daily News*).

A trap was devised for this irresistible intruder, "destined to take the very highest rank" (*Graphic*). That snare was to induce the stranger, if possible, to attempt such exacting character as Lady Macbeth, for example. One averred that she is fitted for more heroic creations than that of Pauline, another that "in the direction of high tragedy, her real genius may found," and that "the actress has been moulded for sterner work than in the outwardly ever-varying Pauline, who invariably never varies at all." If, instead of eclipsing contemporary actresses in the parts they fondly hugged as their own, Miss Anderson had been thus misled, and though she had *succeeded* in some arduous character far and away above their abilities, these would have been tranquil as, had she fallen short of the popular standard, they would have been gleeful.

Therefore, there was gnashing of teeth, more or less false, when, instead of Lady Macbeth, Brutus's wife, Cleopatra, or even Juliet, the modern and not "strong" Galatea was announced for

The Third Impersonation.

Our actress was known throughout London after Sept. 1st (Parthenia) and throughout England after Nov. 27th (Pauline), and the much derided "worn and faded repertory" had in no wise abated that public curiosity which crammed the Lyceum to the back and ceiling, a furore "not to be set down to fashion or caprice" (*News*), adopting the exceptional actress new in her style, marvellous gifted by nature and cultivated to the very limit of art" (*Society*.)   Cultivated! mark that ye false Americans who repeat that no good can come out of Nazareth.

Expectation was piqued by rumors that some inimical influence was busy with Mr. Gilbert to induce him to withhold his mythological comedy from "that Yankee girl."   Whatever the hindrance, the American admirers of the talented author of the "Pinafore" may be sure that Mr. Gilbert was not to blame.   A little soured by hardship at a period of life when his quite evident powers should have been fostered and not exploited ruthlessly*, Mr. Gilbert has a brusqueness of manner which does his real temperament injustice, but he is utterly incapable of unfairness, consequently "Pygmalion and Galatea" was re-introduced under his superintendence.

As for his "revengeful schemes (resentful?)" to come out even because he had never been paid for the piece in America, why he is a lawyer and, therefore, perfectly well knows that he has not the shadow of a claim to a dollar there for playing rights.   The piece is derisely accounted "clumsy and silly and farcial" and the sweetest and most interesting of Mr. Gibert's strange conceptions.   There was one thing accepted beforehand, that this most delicate character would be beautifully embodied as never before (*Vanity Fair*), and necessarily, the original impersonator, Mrs. Kendal, however good in making the statue transform itself into a contemporary English woman would be

---

*For weeks when the proprietor of a comic weekly under his charge paid nobody, Mr. Gilbert toiled loyally for its subscribers, not only writing every line but drawing every picture from the initial to the tailpiece, including the full page cartoon. The writer has handled the copy.

relegated to the base of the pedestal if not expunged from the niche where the Greek image is revealed.

One critic (G. A. Sala,) frankly observed that, having praised Mrs. Kendal as the best Galatea, he would not eat his words! but the other ancient and valiant Pistols masticated their leeks with tolerable gusto. For ourselves, we think Madame Marie Cabel in Masse's opera, was a finer and more antique statue humanized than any seen before Miss Anderson's, and the French prima donna's exposition of the thrill of life and the sensations of vinous effects surpassed even that of the dansense Madame Dos (in "Babil and Bijou").

Of the two readings, the marble to remain an unearthly being when animated, or to become utterly a guileless but feeling woman, Miss Anderson chose to the higher one—" the true one, cool and calm." (*Truth.*)

When the screen glided aloof, the ravished audience was spellbound before "a living statue of really super natural loveliness, expectations being fully realised." (*Referee.*)

All the lighter touches were relished, the innocent gladness, the never undue archness, and the absence of posing for sheer effect.

Some of the purblind actually insisted that this "most faultless of Grecian statues" was a dummy —moulded by Alma-Tadema, although the clearer eye discerned the acceleration of the breathing-pace at the shout of joyful approbation. Then, because the Anglo-French artist named went round to the stage to suggest some trivial alteration of the costume, cavillers hastened to attribute the design to him, though it is the work of Mr. Frank Millet of the city of New York.*

This time, there were less fault-finders. Mr. Gilbert "trimmed" sagely by pronouncing that this best impersonation to then was "artistically more beautiful but dramatically less effective than Mrs. Kendal's." The *Times* rated this new Galatea "ideally beautiful and a totally complete embodiment; the finest *tableau vivant* the stage has ever seen" to "the unbounded admiration of the house." *Truth* called it an interesting and original rendering. (Mrs. Labouchere, at the elbow of her husband thus reviewing, ought to be a judge of statuesque players as she once made up for the popular "Clytie" in a play of that title.) Miss Anderson has proved that grace may be nature, and that finished art is the highest form of grace. A legitimate triumph.

---

*Miss LEMON, daughter of Charles Dickens' early boon-companion and editor of "Punch," wrote these verses to Roekel's melody

GALATEA.

Alone the worker stood and gazed upon that face,
Where all the grace of maidenhood had found a resting-place;
His heart was moved to tears, his soul was moved to pray
"Give me the love of her living heart to crown my life alway."

Across the noontide light a gentle whisper came,
With voice half hushed by tears he heard her breathe his name.
He knew the prayer was heard before the love-queen's throne:
"Thought of my thought, soul of my soul, she lives for my
     love alone!"

Across the after years he listens all in vain
To hear the one loved voice speak to his heart again;
Only a memory lives of all the past could tell,
For all his hope and all his love lie in one word—"Farewell!"

" Rarely, indeed (says the *News*) can an attempt to satisfy by actual bodily presentment the ideal of a poetic legend have approached so nearly to absolute perfection;" adding that her acting, "like all acting that is good, is highly artificial ; but if justifiably stigmatised as artificial, it is devoutly to be wished that such artificiality were more commonly to be met upon our stage. The frank joyousness of 'I am glad I am a woman !' went to the heart."

Though, then, "the critics are always opposed to new and natural readings (in the words of Chorley, head of the London critics himself at one time), the *Observer* concluded that a sculptured figure suddenly endowed with life would comport itself after the fashion of Miss Anderson," the *Academy* that the interpretation of the feelings of a woman not developed and with the coldness of marble still clinging, is very likely original and no doubt justified, and the *Graphic* that "it is difficult to imagine how the realization could be more perfect."

Up to the wierd farewell in a tone of rich, subdued pathos, there had been "nothing to blame and very much to praise " (*Standard*).

The aristocratic *Post*, alluding to the Lyceum magnet as "the fashion," acknowledged that she must be clever as well as fortunate to have attained this result in so short a time. To cap the climax, the court sculptor, Count Gleichen, executed the lady's bust.

Unable to believe that, in competition with native talent, the invader could be defeated, for already her promised Juliet was anticipated as a sure success, a social entanglement was invented to which the public remained totally indifferent. When the Duke of Albany's funeral took place, there was no closing order issued to theatrical managers (who are licensed by the Lord Chamberlain though there is no knowing that he dare cancel the document and throw out a thousand employees on a mere matter of court etiquette), but several houses did make holiday. The Lyceum management, however, was cunningly prompted, advantage being taken of ignorance of London "flunkeyism," not only to go on as usual but publish a kind of democratic appeal to the people that there was no desire to disappoint them. Better advised by sojourners who understood the attempt to injure the actress in the higher circles, who are nothing if not loyal, the performance was put off and Windsor Castle remained unshaken.

Whilst the Shakesperian novelty was in preparation Mr. Gilbert's one act costume comedy was brought out on Jan. 26th, 1884. Meanwhile the year closed gratifying, honorably, profitably. The "quiet" Anderson equipage, with driver and man in dark brown and dead silver buttons, was the very opposite in taste to the circus-like equipage in which one whom the Londoners once took for an "American actress" (Adah Isaacs Menken), used to parade herself in the fashionable West End. The Lyceum company were lavishly remembered at Christmas and, in responsive good feeling, they presented their principal with a brooch in diamonds, ever conspicuous among her stage keepsakes. There was also a feast to some hundred hungry children given by the lady in the notorious Seven Dials, all now that the New York Five Points used to be. By the end of the seven months engagement, nearly $ 500,000 was to pass through the Lyceum treasury! Morever, to say nothing of a myriad copies of American photographs, some thirty thousand, were disposed

of by Vanderweyde (the American artist who has taken
the place of Sarony in the British capital), in whose
studio was also shown the curious carbon photograph
8 x 3 feet, which is larger, we believe, than even those
life-sized ones of Parisian favorites to which M. Nadar
so proudly called our attention a short time since.

Nevertheless, there was one drop of gall in the
beaker of honey ; still some grumblers, in this Land
where Grumbler is King, repeated : " She has come as
a beauty, she has shown herself as living statuary, she
has colored herself with evanescent passion so as to be
a painting of *Pauline ;* now let us see her alive in
drama."

Accordingly, she returned after the holidays to be
no longer the picture, but the artiste in

"Comedy and Tragedy."

A one-act piece written expressly by the now enthusiastic Gilbert to reveal the powers of moving all hearts.

The Fourth Phase.

This " show " play had been bandied about for a doz-
en years : written for Kate Terry, she was rather in
the toils of Tom Taylor who composed nearly every
original play she appeared in, being part proprietor of
the theatre where she was longest engaged, it was offered afterwards to her sister Ellen, who shirked the
arduous task, and to Miss Litton, also prudently declining. The actress's powers are supremely called
upon in the culmination where the heroine, reciting
for the amusement of some court fops, suddenly believes that her beloved husband is being killed in a

duel. She refused to wear powder, and her own brown hair was puffed up in a reasonable imitation of the head-dress of the Regency. Her costume was neither stiff nor voluminous enough for correctness, but, compensation enough to the ladies' eyes, it was deluged with rivers of diamonds. The first thrill was given when her lower tones deeply thundered the rebuke on the status of actors before the Revolution:

"What are we actresses?" "Bodies we have, God help us; souls, we have none. Banned by the church, shunned by the pure, buried like dogs."

In the scene of entanglement with the Prince Regent, to be detained by pretended endearments until the avenging husband arrives, the revelation of a new phase in the siren's abilities surprised all spectators. But, (as Mr. Yates wrote to a New York paper) "Astonishment gave way to admiration in the great scene of the play. The husband and Regent are fighting in a moonlight glade. Clarice diverts her guests attention by enacting the part of a strolling player who has been all things in his time. She is a miser, gloating over his wealth; she is a lover, singing to his lute; she is a gallant, dancing a fandango. She is everything by turns, and played all parts with a skill so consummate that the theatre rang with thunders of applause. In the final scene, where she implores her guests to save her husband's life and they still believe she is acting a part, she never falls into an excess of vehemence, never sins by exaggeration; and at the end of the play, folded in her husband's arms, she gives a long, ominous glance toward the glade where the Regent lies dying: with that glance admirably closes the drama. Indeed, there is not a blemish in this remarkable performance."

The *Athenæum*: "her performance is remarkable for power as for beauty, and holds forth promise of higher things in store. It was to her warmest admirers a a surprise." *Queen*, termed it "a superb display of histrionic skill while she was really acting mimic parts to her audience on the stage."

The *Referee* asserted that the arch and mischievous tone adopted in the comedy lines has never been surpassed.

And the *Academy* thinks "Miss Anderson shows more real power in the comedy line than in Mr. Gilbert's mythological play, and asserts that she adds to the possession of charm much experience and serviceable tact."

Granted, at last that by her talent, as by her beauty, and faultless private life, she was worthy to represent the great country that gave her birth, Miss Anderson could, without misgivings as to the confounded if not crushed enemies behind, go on a triumphal

Tour of Great Britain.

The progress made the starlight fall on smoky Birmingham, bustling Glasgow, stern Edinboro' and noisy Manchester. The prices were those which had distinguished her town season, and achieved a similarly brilliant success. Only once did she disappoint an always eager audience, and that was at Glasgow, where the Scotch mist had given her a cold. They were very much astonished in the Northern Capital by her conscientiousness in having a scene of "Ingomar" gone over several times till it went smoothly. In June the St. Pancras railway station was mobbed by her welcome-makers, whose only chance was to see her on the way to study Juliet in Verona itself.

"Romeo and Juliet."

When Charlotte Cushman, well informed on the machinations of rival tragediennes to prevent her obtaining even one hearing in London, told a manager that she would stay till she overcame those enemies, the echo of her vigorous menace fluttered the foe considerably. The gradual strengthening of Miss Anderson's popularity silenced nearly all opposition, and, unless she were tried by some hypercritical guage, no one in the overflowing audience at the Lyceum, Nov. 1st, 1884, doubted that the new Juliet would occupy no lower a niche in Fame's temple that Adelina Patti, and a higher one than Neilson, Terry, Cavendish, Wallis and the flock comprehensively styled, from their teacher, "Ryder's pupils."

"It gave complete satisfaction to her admirers (says the *Dispatch*), this personation of a more trying and poetical character than any she has previously attempted here." The begrudgeful *Daily Telegraph* owns that "technically speaking a more powerful bit of acting the modern stage has not seen from an English speaking actress!" And what in the name of insatiable Thersites, can one demand further. It is useless to add more of the euloge abounding in the London papers; the audience cheered with a kind of gratefulness at having them for their representatives the Royal party (Prince and Princess of Wales and the Princess Louise of Lorne) who presented their bouquets to our best and fairest actress.

The Correspondents of the American papers flashed their plaudits by telegraph, and their unpremeditated language gives a faithful expression of the impression made:

The long awaited revival of "Romeo and Juliet" with Mr. Terriss and Miss Mary Anderson in the title *rôles* began Nov. 1st at the Lyceum Theatre. The revival was an artistic surprise. The *mise en scene* was historically accurate, with no straining after effect. The faction fight between the Montagues and Capulets in the first act was as wonderful a realization of a street battle in old Verona as ever was displayed on the stage. The entrance of the heroine in this act was the signal for a tremendous burst of enthusiasm. Mary Anderson was never seen to such advantage in London before.

She wore a dress of pale blue Indian silk, delicately figured with silver. The dress was woven all in one piece and was just sufficiently tight-fitting to show to advantage the lines of the actress's classic figure. It had a border of seed pearls and a band of the same ornaments over the hips, while from her wrist, in the ballroom scene, hung a mask at the end of a string of pearl beads. She wore no jewels, and was content to dispense with the ordinary Juliet wig. Her own hair was worn flowing over her shoulders and surmounted by a tiny skull cap of the same material as the dress. Miss Anderson's second costume consisted of a bodice and skirt of heavy apricot satin, with a semi-train, all embroidered with seed pearls and silver. As in the first act, she wore no jewels, but this time her hair was adorned with violets and primroses.

In the action of the piece there were many innovations and departures from London stage traditions.

The house was crowded. The audience included scores of critics and hundred notabilities in social and official life. Among them was Mr. Lowell. There were also many other Americans present. The applause throughout the evening was liberal and appreciative. In the balcony scene the full depth of the stage was used and the setting superb. Miss Anderson was much applauded and twice called before the curtain. The potion scene was finely done, and at the end of the play Miss Anderson was called for with a degree of fervor that admitted of no refusal. She was led before the curtain. The applause at her appearance was tumultous and so prolonged that Miss Anderson retired in tears and blushes, and the orchestra had to play "Home, Sweet Home" to the full strength of their instruments to get the people out of the house.

The general opinion is that Miss Anderson's Juliet is a scholarly and artistic study. She introduced much new business, but it has all been conscientiously considered and appears warranted by the text. She seems to rely chiefly upon facial expression for the portrayal of passion or love.

Miss Mary Anderson's *Juliet* (says the correspondent of the *N. Y. Herald*) seems to have rivalled Mr. Wilson Barrett's Hamlet. It captured a London audience at Mr. Irving's theatre. There is some oddity in this foreign appreciation of an actress less heartly recognized in her own country. Miss Anderson was always a handsome woman, and showed unmistakable signs of a nascent talent. Yet she was never petted here as she is petted in England. This is not uncommon on the stage. Many French actresses go abroad to acquire their fame. Deslée won her laurels in Belgium after Paris had left her in neglect. Pasca made her greatest reputation in Russia. Actors like Fechter. highly esteemed both here and in London, have been very light-

ly considered in France. There is a distinct utility,
however, in this verdict of foreigners. It enables us
to reconsider our own. So Miss Anderson, we suppose,
will come back to us with quite a regal triumph.

Everybody went to see Miss Mary Anderson's first
night of "Romeo and Juliet." All Mr. Irving's friends
were there, Mr. Herrmann representing his rival of the
Princess's Theatre. His Excellency Minister Lowell,
Mrs. Lowell, and Mr. Smalley, of the *Tribune*, occupied
a box. Mr. McHenry, the Financist, and some friends
were in the next one. George H. Boughton, the American artist, Mrs. Boughton, Mr. Abbey, of *Harper's*,
Sala, Mr. and Mrs. Labouchere, Mr. Justin McCarthy,
M. P., Mrs. Lewis and two other sisters of Ellen Terry,
Mr. and Mrs. Ledger, Mr. Burnand, editor of *Punch*,
and Mrs. Burnand, Dr. Morrell Mackenzie, and all the
leading critics, were in the stalls. It was a thoroughly
representative house, great in its expectations, anxious
to be pleased and willing to see the high traditions of
the Lyceum management maintained. It is conceded
in cultured circles that Mary Anderson has been more
sincere in her respect and veneration for Shakespeare;
that she has approached the poet in a more poetic spirit;
and that she has not, for a moment, lowered his work
to the level of mere melodrama. Mary Anderson's
Juliet was a surprise, even to her admirers. It is a
great advance on all she has done before. Bright, fresh,
artless, coquettish in the earlier scenes, it was strong,
womanly and dramatic at the close. It was never uninteresting and it was always conscientious and earnest.
No handsomer young couple ever beguiled an audience of its sympathy than did the *Juliet* of Miss An-

derson and the *Romeo* of Mr. Terris. The beau ideal
of the Shakesperean picture, they will never be forgotten in the oral history of the famous balcony scene.
Tybalt was admirably played by one of Miss Anderson's
brothers. Mrs. Stirling (the nurse of the Irving rep-
resentation) gave great satisfaction in all her scenes,
and Miss Anderson was perhaps at her best in the
comedy passages with the nurse; though Mrs. Keely
and Mr. Robert Wyndham (two theatrical authorities)
say they never saw the potion scene given with such
true tragic fire as on Saturday night. The scenery was
superb. If it had a fault it was too lavish; and it
certainly did not possess that poetic glamor with which
Irving succeeded in investing his version of the immortal
story. Nevertheless the scenes were very effective,
and they evidently afforded a real delight to the more
popular parts of the house. This latest venture of Mr.
Abbey and Miss Anderson may honestly be pronounced
a genuine artistic and money success.

————◆————

Miss Mary Anderson has herself personally inves-
tigated the real and supposed scenes of "Juliet and her
Romeo." And she kept her eyes wide open for local
color and suggestive incident, it seems, in Verona.
"Carados," the bright and incisive gossip of the *London
Referee*, informs me that "while inspiration seeking in
this classic Italian city, she saw a band of barefooted
ecclesiastics solemnly march through the streets.
Gibbon you know, saw something of the same kind
years ago at Rome. " The effect on Miss Anderson
will be seen when, the play will be produced." Miss
Anderson superintends the rehearsals with a watchful
energy that leaves no effect. grouping, or situation un-

explored. A hundred and eighty supers are daily
drilled for the fighting and banquet scenes, both of
which are to be "something very remarkable." It is
understood that this new mounting of "Romeo and
Juliet" is not intended for England alone. Mr. Abbey
and Miss Anderson have in view for it a great American tour.

By the Sad Sea Waves.

A correspondent of a London paper, gives the following sketch of Miss Anderson, "at home."

"A long low room in a rambling country house, its
wide bay windows commanding the pretty wooded
scenery of Long Branch. The golden rays pour in
through the open windows, and fill the room with splendor. The walls are covered with portraits of eminent
actors and actresses, living and dead: here and there a
bust or statuette, a stage dagger on a velvet stand which
once belonged to Sarah Siddons; while on chairs and
sofas are lying editions of Shakespeare, and of the
works of many another playwright. Seated at an organ
is a young woman in the bloom of a singular beauty.
She is dressed in a soft white cashmere robe, whose
clinging folds display the graceful outlines of her full
supple form. She wears no ornament, and the sim-
plicity of her attire is only relieved by the broad sash
of pale-blue silk which encircles her yielding waist.
The sunbeams fall upon a face of singular loveliness,
features exquisitely chiselled, a small finely-shaped head
carried with a queenly grace and lit up with deep-gray
eyes full of mingled genius and passion. This head

is crowned with a wealth of that seldom-seen hair—
"Golden in the sunshine, in the shadow brown." Presently the lady commences to sing in a sweet, powerful
contralto voice. She has scarcely uttered a few notes
when a large English deerhound who has been dozing
quietly at her feet starts up, and after a long preliminary stretch commences a doleful accompaniment.
She leaves the organ, and administering to Uno a re
proachful slap, bids him be quiet. The spell is broken.
In a moment we are in the nineteenth century, at a
country house at one of America's most fashionable
watering-places; and the beautiful young woman before us is Mary Anderson, the glory of the American
stage, and one of the fairest daughters of that fair land.
This is the home to which she retires now and then
for a few weeks rest and quiet from the exacting life of
a successful actress, whose days are spent in nomadic
pursuit of her professor.

"She introduces you presently to the family circle.
The introductions are hardly over when Miss Anderson
insists on taking you to the top of the house, whose
windows command a fine view of the Atlantic, as it rolls
majestically on to the shore of Long Branch. Miss
Anderson points out to you her bathing-place at the
foot of the park. An expert and adventurous swimmer,
she will rush down sometimes on a sultry summer's
night, and plunge, under the bright moonlit sky, into
angry waters, which one less courageous might well
fear to breast; and there in the offing is her pretty
steam-yacht, in which she often flies seawards, to escape for a few days 'far from the madding crowd' of
Long Branch."

SELECT RECITATIONS.

EXECUTION OF MARY STUART.

Barbara.   Yea, I see
Stand in mid-hall the scaffold black as death.
And black the block upon it all around.
Against the throng a guard of halberdiers,
And the axe against the scaffold rail reclined,
And two men masked on either hand beyond,
And hard behind the block a cushion set,
Black, as the chair behind it.
  Mary Beaton.   When I saw
Fallen on a scaffold once a young man's head,
Such things as these I saw not. Nay, but on:
I knew not that I spake: and toward your ears
Indeed I spake not.
  Barbara.   All those faces change;
She comes more royally than ever yet
Fell foot of man triumphant on this earth,
Imperial more than empire made her born
Enthroned as queen sat never. Not a line
Stirs of her sovereign feature: like a bride
Brought home she mounts the scaffold; and her eyes
Sweep regal round the cirque beneath, and rest,
Subsiding with a smile. She sits, and they,
The doomsmen earls, beside her; at her left
The sheriff, and the clerk at hand on high,
To read the warrant.
  Mary Beaton.   None stands there but knows

What things therein are writ against her: God
Knows what therein is writ not. God forgive
All.
  Barbara. Not a face there breathes of all the throng
But is more moved than hers to hear this read,
Whose look alone is changed not.
  Mary Beaton.   Once I knew
A face that changed not in as dire an hour
More than the queen's face changes. Hath he not
Ended?
  Barbara. You cannot hear them speak below:
Come near and hearken: bid not me repeat
All.
  Mary Beaton. I beseech you—for I may not come.
  Barbara. Now speaks Lord Shrewsbury but a word
          or twain,
And brieflier yet she answers, and stands up
As though to kneel, and pray.
  Mary Beaton.   I too have prayed—
God hear at last her prayers not less than mine,
Which failed not, sure, of hearing.
          *   *   *   *   *   *   *   *   *

  Barbara. And now they lift her veil up from her head.
Softly and softly draw the black robe off,
And all in red as of a funeral flame
She stands up statelier yet before them, tall,
And clothed as if with sunset; and she takes
From Elspeth's hands the crimson sleeves, and draws
Their covering on her arms, and now those twain
Burst out aloud in weeping; and she speaks:
Weep not; I promised for you. Now she kneels;
And Jane binds round a kerchief on her eyes:
And smiling last her heavenliest smile on earth,
She waves a blind hand toward them, with *Farewell,*
Farewell, to meet again: and they come down
And leave her praying aloud, *In thee, O Lord,*
I put my trust: and now, that psalm being through,
She lays between the block and her soft neck
Her long white peerless hands up tenderly,
Which now the headsman draws again away,

But softly too : now stir her lips again—
Into thine hands, O Lord, into thine hands,
Lord, I commend my spirit : and now—but now.
Look you, not I, the last upon her.
    Mary Beaton.   Ha!
He strikes awry ; she stirs not.   Nay, but now
He strikes aright, and ends it.
    Barbara.   Hark, a cry.
Voice below.   So perish all found enemies of the Queen!
Another Voice.   Amen.
    Mary Beaton.   I heard that very cry go up
Far off long since to God, who answers here.

SWINBURNE.

———•———

"BY THE SEA, SEPTEMBER 19, 1881."

    Watchman! what of the night?
The sky is dark, my friend,
And we in heavy grief await the end.
A light is burning in a silent room,
But we—we have no light in all the gloom.

    Watchman! what of the night?
Friend, strong men watch the light
With the strange mist of tears before their sight,
And women at each hearthstone sob and pray
That the great darkness end at last in day.

    Watchman! how goes the night?
Wearily, friend, for him,
Yet his heart quails not, though the light burns dim.
As bravely as he fought the field of life,
He bears himself in this, the final strife.

    Watchman! what of the night?
Friend, we are left no word
To tell of all the bitter sorrow stirred

In our sad souls.   We stand and rail at fate
Who leaves hands empty and hearts desolate.

" Are pure, great souls so many in the land
That we should lose the chosen of the band ? "
We cry !   But he who suffers lies,
Meeting sharp-weaponed pain with steadfast eyes

And makes no plaint while on the threshold death
Half draws his keen sword from its glittering sheath
And looking inward pauses—lingering long,
Faltering—himself the weak before the strong.

Watchman ! how goes the night ?
In tears, my friend, and praise
Of his high truth and generous, trusting ways ;
Of his warm love and buoyant hope and faith
Which passed life's fires free from all blight or scathe.
Strange ! we forget the laurel wreath we gave,
And only love him, standing near his grave.

Watchman ! what of the night ?
Friend, when it is past,
We wonder what our grief can bring at last,
To lay upon his broad, true, tender breast,
What flower whose sweetness shall outlast the rest,
And this we set from all the bloom apart ;
" He woke new love and faith in every heart."

Watchman ! what of the night?
Would God that it were gone
And we might see once more the rising dawn !
The darkness deeper grows—the light burns low,
There sweeps o'er land and sea a cry of woe !

Watchman ! What now ! What now !
Hush, friend—we may not say,
Only that—all the pain has passed away.

MRS. FRANCES HODGSON BURNETT.

THE BALCONY SCENE.

ROMEO AND JULIET.——Act II.—Scene 2.

Romeo. He jests at scars that never felt a wound.
     [*Juliet appears above at a window.*
But, soft! what light through yonder window breaks?
It is the east, and Juliet is the sun.
See, how she leans her cheek upon her hand!
O, that I were a glove upon that hand,
That I might touch that cheek!
 Juliet.   Ay me!
 Rom.   She speaks;
O, speak again, bright angel! for thou art
As glorious to this night, being o'er my head,
As is a winged messenger of heaven
Unto the white upturned wondering eyes
Of mortals that fall back to gaze on him
When he bestrides the lazy-pacing clouds
And sails upon the bosom of the air.
 Jul. O Romeo, Romeo! wherefore art thou Romeo?
Deny thy father and refuse thy name;
Or, if thou wilt not, be but sworn my love,
And I'll no longer be a Capulet.
 Rom. [*Aside*] Shall I hear more, or shall I speak
  at this?
 Jul. 'Tis but thy name that is my enemy;
Thou art thyself, though not a Montague.
What's Montague? it is nor hand nor foot,
Nor arm, nor face, nor any other part

Belonging to a man.   O, be some other name!
What's in a name? that which we call a rose
By any other name would smell as sweet;
So Romeo would, were he not Romeo call'd,
Retain that dear perfection which he owes
Without that title, Romeo, doff thy name,
And for that name which is no part of thee
Take all myself.
 Rom.   I take thee at thy word:
Call me but love, and I'll be new baptized;
Henceforth I never will be Romeo.   [night,
 Jul. What man art thou that thus bescreen'd in
So stumblest on my counsel?
 Rom.   By a name
I know not how to tell thee who I am:
My name, dear saint, is hateful to myself,
Because it is an enemy to thee;
Had I it written, I would tear the word.
 Jul. My ears have not yet drunk a hundred words
Of that tongue's utterance, yet I know the sound:
Art thou not Romeo and a Montague?
 Rom. Neither, fair saint, if either thee dislike.
 Jul. How camest thou hither, tell me, and wherefore?
The orchard walls are high and hard to climb,
And the place death, considering who thou art,
If any of my kinsmen find thee here. [walls.
 Rom. With love's light wings did I o'er perch these
For stony limits cannot hold love out,
And what love can do that dares love attempt;
Therefore thy kinsmen are no let to me.
 Jul. If they do see thee, they will murder thee.
 Rom. Alack, there lies more peril in thine eye
Than twenty of their swords: look thou but sweet,
And I am proof against their enmity.
 Jul. I would not for the world they saw thee here.
 Rom. I have night's cloak to hide me from their
  sight;
And but thou love me, let them find me here:
My life were better ended by their hate.
Than death prorogued, wanting of thy love.

Jul. By who's direction found'st thou out this place?

Rom. By love, who first did prompt me to inquire;
He lent me counsel and I lent him eyes.
I am no pilot; yet, wert thou as far
As that vast shore wash'd with the farthest sea,
I would adventure for such merchandise.

Jul. Thou know'st the mask of night is on my face,
Else would a maiden blush bepaint my cheek
For that which thou has heard me speak to night.
Fain would I dwell on form, fain, fain deny
What I have spoke: but farewell compliment!
Dost thou love me? I know thou wilt say "Ay,"
And I will take thy word: yet, if thou swear'st,
Thou mayst prove false; at lovers' perjuries,
They say, Jove laughs. O gentle Romeo,
If thou dost love, pronounce it faithfully:
Or if thou think'st I am too quickly won,
I'll frown and be perverse and say thee nay,
So thou wilt woo; but else, not for the world.
In truth, fair Montague, I am too fond,
And therefore thou mayst think my 'haviour light:
But trust me, gentleman, I'll prove more true
Than those that have more cunning to be strange.
I should have been more strange, I must confess,
But that thou overheard'st, ere I was ware,
My true love's passion: therefore pardon me,
And not impute this yielding to light love,
Which the dark night hath so discovered.

Rom. Lady, by yonder blessed moon I swear
That tips with silver all these fruit-tree tops—

Jul. O, swear not by the moon, the inconstant moon,
That monthly changes in her circled orb,
Lest that thy love prove likewise variable.

Rom. What shall I swear by?

Jul.   Do not swear at all;
Or, if thou wilt, swear by thy gracious self,
Which is the god of my idolatry,
And I'll believe thee.

Rom.   If my heart's dear love—

Jul. Well, do not swear: although I joy in thee,
I have no joy of this contract to-night:
It is too rash, too unadvised, too sudden;
Too like the lightning, which doth cease to be
Ere one can say "It lightens." Sweet, good night!
This bud of love, by summer's ripening breath,
May prove a beauteous flower when next we meet.
Good night, good night! as sweet repose and rest
Come to thy heart as that within my breast!
  Rom. O, wilt thou leave me so unsatisfied?
  Jul. What satisfaction canst thou have to-night?
  Rom. The exchange of thy love's faithful vow for
    mine.
  Jul. I gave thee mine before thou didst request it:
And yet I would it were to give again.   [love?
  Rom. Wouldst thou withdraw it? for what purpose,
  Jul. But to be frank, and give it thee again,
And yet I wish but for the thing I have:
My bounty is as boundless as the sea.
My love as deep; the more I give to thee,
The more I have, for both are infinite.
                              [*Nurse calls within.*
I hear some noise within; dear love, adieu!
Anon, good nurse! Sweet Montague, be true.
Stay but a little, I will come again.   [*Exit, above.*
  Rom. O blessed, blessed night! I am afeard,
Being in night, all this is but a dream,
Too flattering-sweet to be substantial.

                Re-enter Juliet, *above.*

  Jul. Three words, dear Romeo, and good night
    indeed.
If that thy bent of love be honorable.
Thy purpose marriage, send me word to-morrow,
By one that I'll procure to come to thee,
Where and what time thou wilt perform the rite;
And all my fortunes at thy foot I'll lay
And follow thee my lord throughout the world.
  Nurse. [*Within*] Madam!
  Jul. I come anon.—But if thou mean'st not well,

I do beseech thee—
Nurse. [*Within*] Madam!
Jul.   By and by, I come :—
To cease thy suit, and leave me to grief:
To-morrow will I send.
Rom.   So thrive my soul—
Jul. A thousand times good night!   [*Exit, above.*
Rom. A thousand times the worse, to want thy light.
Love goes toward love, as schoolboys from their books,
But love from love, toward school with heavy looks.
                                [*Retiring.*

      Re-enter Juliet, *above.*

Jul. Hist! Romeo, hist! O, for a falconer's voice,
To lure this tassel-gentle back again!
Bondage is hoarse, and may not speak aloud;
Else would I tear the cave where Echo lies,
And make her airy tongue more hoarse than mine,
With repetition of my Romeo's name.
Rom. It is my soul that calls upon my name:
How silver sweet sound lovers' tongues by night,
Like softest music to attending ears!
Jul. Romeo!
Rom.   My dear?
Jul.   At what o'clock to-morrow
Shall I send to thee?
Rom.   At the hour of nine.
Jul. I will not fail: 'tis twenty years till then.
I have forgot why I did call thee back.
Rom. Let me stand here till thou remember it.
Jul. I shall forget, to have thee still stand there,
Remembering how I love thy company.
Rom. And I'll still stay, to have thee still forget,
Forgetting any other home but this.
Jul. 'Tis almost morning; I would have thee gone:
And yet no further than a wanton's bird;
Who lets it hop a little from her hand,
Like a poor prisoner in his twisted gyves,
And with a silk thread plucks it back again,

So loving-jealous of his liberty.
  Rom. I would I were thy bird.
  Jul.   Sweet, so would I:
Yet I should kill thee with much cherishing.
Good night, good night! parting is such sweet sorrow,
That I shall say good night till it be morrow.
                                    [*Exit above.*
  Rom. Sleep dwell upon thine eyes, peace in thy
     breast!
Would I were sleep and peace, so sweet to rest!
Hence will I to my ghostly father's cell,
His help to crave, and my dear hap to tell.

                              SHAKESPEARE.

THE GRIEF OF CONSTANCE.

KING JOHN.——Act III—Scene 4.

Enter CONSTANCE.

  Constance. Lo, now! now see the issue of your
     peace.
  King Philip. Patience, good lady! comfort, gen-
     tle Constance!
  Const. No, I defy all counsel, all redress,
But that which ends all counsel, true redress,
Death, death; O amiable lovely death!
Thou odoriferous stench, sound rottenness!
Arise forth from the couch of lasting night,
Thou hate and terror to prosperity,
And I will kiss thy detestable bones
And put my eyeballs in thy vaulty brows,
And ring these fingers with thy household worms,
And stop this gap of breath with fulsome dust
And be a carrion monster like thyself:
Come, grin on me, and I will think thou smilest

And buss thee as thy wife.   Misery's love,
O, come to me!
   K. Phi.   O fair affliction, peace!
   Const.   No, no, I will not, having breath to cry:
O, that my tongue were in the thunder's mouth!
Then with a passion would I shake the world;
And rouse from sleep that fell anatomy
Which cannot hear a lady's feeble voice,
Which scorns a modern invocation.   [row.
   Pandulph. Lady, you utter madness, and not sor-
   Const. Thou art not holy to belie me so;
I am not mad: this hair I tear is mine;
My name is Constance; I was Geffrey's wife;
Young Arthur is my son, and he is lost;
I am not mad: I would to heaven I were!
For then, 'tis like I should forget myself:
O, if I could, what grief should I forget!
Preach some philosophy to make me mad,
And thou shalt be canonized, cardinal;
For being not mad but sensible of grief,
My reasonable part produces reason
How I may be deliver'd of these woes,
And teaches me to kill or hang myself:
If I were mad, I should forget my son,
Or madly think a babe of clouts were he:
I am not mad; too well, too well I feel
The different plague of each calamity.
   K. Phi. Bind up those tresses. O, what love I note
In the fair multitude of those her hairs!
Where but by chance a silver drop hath fallen
Even to that drop ten thousand wiry friends
Do glue themselves in sociable grief,
Like true, inseparable, faithful loves,
Sticking together in calamity.
   Const. To England, if you will.
   K. Phi.   Bind up your hairs.
   Const. Yes, that I will; and wherefore will I do it?
I tore them from their bonds and cried aloud
"O that these hands could so redeem my son,
As they have given these hairs their liberty!"

But now I envy at their liberty,
And will again commit them to their bonds,
Because my poor child is a prisoner.
And, father cardinal, I have heard you say
That we shall see and know our friends in heaven:
If that be true, I shall see my boy again;
For since the birth of Cain, the first male child,
To him that did but yesterday suspire,
There was not such a gracious creature born
But now will canker-sorrow eat my bud
And chase the native beauty from his cheek
And he will look as hollow as a ghost,
As dim and meagre as an ague's fit.
And so he'll die; and, rising so again,
When I shall meet him in the court of heaven
I shall not know him: therefore never, never
Must I behold my pretty Arthur more.

Pand. You hold too heinous a respect of grief.
Const. He talks to me that never had a son.
K. Phi. You are as fond of grief as of your child.
Const. Grief fills the room up of my absent child,
Lies in his bed, walks up and down with me,
Puts on his pretty looks, repeats his words,
Remembers me of all his gracious parts,
Stuffs out his vacant garments with his form;
Then, have I reason to be fond of grief?
Fare you well: had you such a loss as I,
I could give better comfort than you do.
I will not keep this form upon my head,
When there is such disorder in my wit.
O Lord! my boy, my Arthur, my fair son!
My life, my joy, my food, my all the world!
My widow-comfort, and my sorrows' cure!

SHAKESPEARE.

A DREAM OF MIRIAM.

Then I heard

A noise of some one coming through the lawn,
And singing clearer than the crested bird,
   That claps his wings at dawn.

"The torrent brooks of hallowed Israel,
   From craggy hollows pouring, late and soon,
Sound all night long, in falling thro' the dell,
   Far-heard beneath the moon.

"The balmy moon of blessed Israel
   Floods all the deep-blue gloom with beams divine:
All night the splintered crags that wall the dell
   With spires of silver shine."

As one that museth where broad sunlight laves
   The lawn by some cathedral, thro' the door
Hearing the holy organ rolling waves
   Of sound on roof and floor.

Within, and anthem sung, is charmed and tied
   To where he stands,—so stood I, when that flow
Of music left the lips of her that died
   To save her father's vow:

The daughter of the warrior Gileadite,
   A maiden pure; as when she went along
From Mizpeth's tower'd gate with welcome light,
With timbrel and with song.

My words leapt forth: "Heaven heads the count of
    crimes
   With that wild oath." She rendered answer high:
"Not so, nor once alone: a thousand times
   I would be born and die.

"Single I grew, like some green plant, whose root
   Creeps to the garden water-pipes beneath,
Feeding the flower; but ere my flower to fruit
   Changed, I was ripe for death.

"My God, my land, my father—these did move
Me from my bliss of life, that nature gave,
Lower'd softly with a threefold cord of love
    Down to a silent grave.

"And I went mourning, "No fair Hebrew boy
    Shall smile away my maiden blame among
The Hebrew mothers'—emptied of all joy,
    Leaving the dance and song.

"Leaving the olive-gardens far below,
    Leaving the promise of my bridal bower,
The valleys of grape-loaded vines that glow
    Beneath the battled tower.

"The light white cloud swam over us. Anon
    We heard the lion roaring from his den;
We saw the large white stars rise one by one,
    Or, from the darken'd glen,

"Saw God divide the night with flying flame,
    And thunder on the everlasting hills.
I heard him, for he spake, and grief became
    A solemn scorn of ills.

"When the next moon was rolled into the sky,
    Strength came to me that equall'd my desire,
How beautiful a thing it was to die
    For God and for my sire!

"It comforts me in this one thought to dwell,
    That I subdued me to my father's will;
Because the kiss he gave me, ere I fell
    Sweetens the spirit still."

    *   *   *   Here her face
    Glowed, as I looked at her.

She locked her lips: she left me where I stood:
    "Glory to God," she sang, and passed afar,
Thridding the sombre boskage of the wood,
    Toward the morning-star.

                                        TENNYSON.

MASTER WALTER'S WARD.

THE HUNCHBACK.——Act I.—Scene 2.

Helen. (L.) I like not, Julia, this, your country life.
I'm weary on't.
 Julia. (R.) Indeed! So am not I!
I know no other; would no other know.   [know
 Helen. You would no other know! Would you not
Another relative?—another friend—
Another house—another anything,
Because the ones you have already please you?
That's poor content! "Would you not be more rich?
"More wise, more fair?" The song that last you learned
You fancy well, and, therefore, shall you learn
No other song? Your virginal, 'tis true,
Hath a sweet tone; but does it follow thence,
You shall not have another virginal?
You *may* love, and a sweeter one, and so
A sweeter life may find, than this you lead!
 Julia. I seek it not. Helen, I'm constancy!
 Helen. So is a cat, a dog, a silly hen,
An owl, a bat—where they are wont to lodge
That still sojourn, nor care to shift their quarters.
Thou'rt constancy? I'm glad I know thy name!
The spider comes of the same family,
That in his meshy fortress spends his life,
Unless you pull it down, and scare him from it.
And so thou'rt constancy? Art proud of that?
And so, in very deed, thou'rt constancy?
 Julia. Helen, you know the adage of the tree—
I've ta'en the bend. This rural life of mine,
Enjoined by an unknown father's will,
I've led from infancy. Debarred from hope
Of change, I ne'er have sighed for change. The town
To me was like the moon, for any thought
I e'er should visit it—nor was I schooled
To think it half so fair!
 Helen.   Not half so fair!

The town's the sun, and thou hast dwelt in night
E'er since thy birth, not to have seen the town!
Their women there are queens, and kings their men;
Their houses palaces! (*crosses*, R.)

   Julia. (*crosses* L.)   And what of that?
Have your town palaces a hall like this?
Couches so fragrant? Walls so high adorned?
Casements with such festoons, such prospects, Helen,
As these fair vistas have? Your kings and queens!
See me a May-day queen, and talk of them.

   Helen. Extremes are never neighbors. 'Tis a step
From one to the other! Were thy constancy
A reasonable thing—a little less
Of constancy—a woman's constancy—
I should not wonder wert thou ten years hence
The maid I know thee now; but as it is,
The odds are ten to one, that this day year
Will see our May-day queen a city one.

   Julia. Never! I'm wedded to a country life.
O, did you hear what Master Walter says?
Nine times in ten the town's a hollow thing,
Where what things are. is naught to what they show;
Where merit's name laughs merit's self to scorn!
Where friendship and esteem, that ought to be
The tenants of men's hearts, lodge in their looks
And tongues alone. Where little virtue, with
A costly keeper, passes for a heap;
A heap for none, that have a homely one!
Where fashion makes the law—your umpire which
You bow to, whether it have brains or not.
Where Folly taketh off his cap and bell,
To clap on Wisdom, which must bear the jest!
Where, to pass current, you must seem the thing,
The passive thing that others think you, and not
Your simple, honest, independent self! (*crosses*, R.)

   Helen. Ay, so says Master Walter. See I not
What you can find in Master Walter, Julia,
To be so fond of him!

   Julia.   He's fond of me!

I've known him since I was a child.   E'en then
The week I thought a weary, heavy one,
That brought not Master Walter.   I had those
About me then that made a fool of me.
As children oft are fooled; but more I loved
Good Master Walter's lesson, than the play
With which they'd surfeit me.   As I grew up,
More frequent Master Walter came, and more
I loved to see him.   I had tutors then,
Men of great skill and learning—but not one   [me,
That taught like Master Walter.   What they'd show
And I, dull as I was, but doubtful saw—
A word from Master Walter made as clear
As daylight.   When my schooling days were o'er—
That's now good three years past—three years—I vow
I'm twenty, Helen—well, as I was saying,
When I had done with school, and all were gone,
Still Master Walter came, and still he comes,
Summer or winter—frost or rain.   I've seen
The snow upon a level with the hedge,
Yet there was Master Walter!

KNOWLES.

THE WIFE'S SUPPLICATION.

FAZIO.——Act IV.—Scene 3.

Enter Aldabella.

Aldabella.   Fazio in prison!   Fazio doom'd to die!—
I was too hasty; should have fled, and bashfully
Beckoned him after; lured him, not seized on him.
Proud Aldabella a poor robber's paramour!
Oh, it sounds dismal!   Florence must not hear it—
And sooth, his time is brief to descant on it.—

Enter Bianca.

And who art thou, thus usherless and unbidden,
Scarest my privacy?
   Bianca. There is one—
Fie, fie upon this choking in my throat—
One thou didst love,—Giraldi Fazio ;—
One who loved thee,—Giraldi Fazio,—
He's doom'd to die, to die to-morrow morning.
Thou'rt high-born, rich and beautiful; the prince,
The prime of Florence wait upon thy smiles,
Like sunflowers on the golden light they love;
Thy lips have such sweet melody, 'tis hung upon
Till silence is an agony. Did it plead
For one condemn'd, but oh, most innocent,
'Twould be a music th' air would fall in love with,
And never let it die till it had won
Its honest purpose.
   Ald. What a wanton waste
Of idle praise is here!
   Bian. Frown not on me:
Thou think'st that he's a murderer—'tis all false;
A trick of Fortune, fancifully cruel,
To cheat the world of such a life as Fazio's.
   Ald. Frivolous and weak: I could not if I would.
   Bian. Nay, but I'll lure thee with so rich a boon—
Hear—hear, and thou art won. If thou dost save him,
It is but just he should be saved for thee.
I give him thee—Bianca—I, his wife—
I pardon all that has been, all that may be—
Oh, I will be thy handmaid ; be so patient—
Calmly, contentedly, and sadly patient—
And if you see a pale or envious motion
Upon my cheek, a quivering on my lips,
Like to complaint—then strike him dead before me.
Thou shalt enjoy all—all that I enjoy'd:—
His love, his life, his sense, his soul be thine;
And I will bless thee, in my misery bless thee.
   Ald. What mist is on my wild and wandering eyes?
Know'st thou to whom and where thou play'st the
      raver?

I, Aldabella, whom the amorous homage
Of rival lords and princes stir no more
Than the light passing of the common air—
I—

   Bian. Proud-lipped woman, earth's most gorgeous
      sovereigns
Were worthless of my Fazio! Foolish woman,
Thou cast'st a jewel off! The proudest lord
That ever revell'd in thy unchaste arms
Was a swarth galley-slave to Fazio.
Ah, me! ah me! e'en I, his lawful wife,
Know't not more truly, certainly than thou.
Hadst thou loved him, I had pardon'd, pitied thee;
We two had sat, all cold, palely sad;
Dropping, like statues on a fountain side,
A pure, a silent, and eternal dew.
Hadst thou outwept me, I had loved thee for't—
And that were easy, for I'm stony here.
               [Putting her hands to her eyes.

   Ald. (*Turning away.*) There is a dizzy trembling
      in mine eye;
But I must dry the foolish dew for shame.
Well, what is it to me? I slew him not;
Nay, nor denounced him to the judgment seat.
I but debase myself to lend free hearing
To such coarse fancies. I must hence, to-night
I feast the lords of Florence.   *[Exit.*

   Bian. They're all lies:
All tales of human goodness! Or they're legends
Left us of some good old forgotten time,
Ere harlotry became a queenly sin,
And housed in palaces. Oh, earth's so crowded
With Vice, that if strange Virtue stray abroad,
They hoot it from them like a thing accurst,
Fazio, my Fazio! but we'll laugh at them:
We will not stay upon their wicked soil,
E'en though they sue us not to die and leave them.

                         MILMAN.

GREEK GIRL AND THE BARBARIAN.

Ingomar. That's good; come, that looks well;
She is a brave girl! she rules herself, and if
She keep her word, we have made a good exchange—
'I'll weep no more.' Aha! I like the girl.
And if——Ho! whither goest thou?
    [*To Parthenia who is going off with two goblets.*
Parthenia. Where should I go? to yonder brook, to
    cleanse the cups.
Ing. No! stay and talk with me.
Par. I have duties to perform.   [*Going*
Ing. Stay—I command you, slave!
Par. I am no slave! your hostage, but no slave.
I go to cleanse the cups. .   [*Exit* L.
Ing. Ho! here's a self-willed thing—here is a spirit!
                [*Mimicking her.*
'I will not, I am no slave! I have duties to perform!
Take me for hostage!' and she flung back her head
As though she brought with her a ton of gold!
'I'll weep no more,'—Aha! an impudent thing.
She pleases me! I love to be opposed;   [snarl,
I love my horse when he rears, my dogs when they
The mountain torrent, and the sea, when it flings
Its foam up to the stars; such things as these
Fill me with life and joy. Tame indolence
Is living death! the battle of the strong
Alone is life!
    [*During this speech Parthenia has returned
    with the cups and a bundle of field flowers.
    She seats herself on a piece of rock in front.*
Ing. Ah! she is here again. (*He approaches her,
and leans over her on the rock.*) What art thou making
    there?
Par. I? garlands.

Ing.   Garlands?

Musing.]   It seems to me as I before had seen her
In a dream! How! Ah, my brother!—he who died
A child—yes, that is it.   My little Folko—
. She has his dark brown hair, his sparkling eye:
Even the voice seems known again to me:
I ll not to sleep—I'll talk to her.   [*Returns to her.*
These you call garlands,
And wherefore do you weave them?

Par. For these cups.

Ing. How?

Par. Is it not with you a custom?   With us
At home, we love to intertwine with flowers,
Our cups and goblets.

Ing. What use is such a plaything?

Par. Use?   They are beautiful; that is their use.
The sight of them makes glad the eye; their scent
Refreshes. cheers.   There
        [*Fastens the half-finished garland round a cup
        and presents it to him.*]   Is not that, now
        beautiful?   [up

Ing. Ay—by the bright sun! That dark green mixed
With the gay flowers! Thou must teach our women
To weave such garlands.

Par. That is soon done: thy wife
Herself shall soon weave wreaths as well as I. [woman

Ing. (*Laughing heartily.*)   My wife! my wife! a
Dost thou say?
I thank the gods, not I.   This is my wife—
            [*Pointing to his accoutrements.*
My spear, my shield, my sword; let him who will
Waste cattle, slaves, or gold, to buy a woman;
Not I—not I!

Par. To buy a woman?—how?

Ing. What is the matter? why dost look so strangely?

Par. How! did I hear aright? bargain for brides
As you would slaves—buy them like cattle?

Ing. Well, I think a woman fit only for a slave.
We follow our own customs, as you yours.
How do you in your city there?   ,

Par.   Consult our hearts.
Massilia free-born daughters are not sold,
But bound by choice with bands as light and sweet
As these I hold.   Love only buys us there.   [bands!
   Ing. Marry for love—what! do you love your hus-
   Par. Why marry else?
   Ing. Marry for love; that's strange!
I cannot comprehend.   I love my horse,
My dogs, my brave companions—but no woman!
What dost thou mean by love—what is it, girl?
   Par. What is it?   'Tis of all things the most sweet—
The heaven of life—or, so my mother says,
I never felt it.
   Ing.   Never?
   Par.   No, indeed.   [*Looking at garland.*
Now look how beautiful!   Here would I wave
Red flowers if I had them.
   Ing.   Yonder there,
In that thick wood they grow
   Par.   How sayest thou?   [some.
(*Looking off.*)   Oh, what a lovely red!   Go pluck me
   Ing. (*Starting at the suggestion.*)   I go for thee?
      the master serve the slave!

                [*Gazing on her with increasing interest·*

And yet, why not? I'll go—the poor child's tired.
   Par. Dost thou hesitate?
   Ing. No, thou shall have the flowers
As fresh and dewy as the bush affords.

                              [*He goes off,* R.

   Par: (*Holding out the wreath.*)
I never yet succeeded half so well.
It will be charming! Charming? and for whom?
Here among savages! no mother here
Looks smiling on it—I am alone, forsaken?
But no, I'll weep no more! No, none shall say I fear.

      Re-enter INGOMAR, *with a bunch of flowers, and
         slowly advancing towards Parthenia.*

Ing. (*Aside.*) The little Folko, when in his play he
  wanted
Flowers or fruit, would so cry 'Bring them to me;
Quick! I will have them—these I will have or none;'
Till somehow he compelled me to obey him,
And she, with the same spirit, the same fire—
Yes there is much of the bright child in her,
Well, she shall be a little brother to me!
There are the flowers.   [*He hands her the flowers.*
  Par. Thanks, thanks. Oh, thou hast broken them
Too short off in the stem
              [*She throws some of them on the ground.*

  Ing. Shall I go and get thee more?
  Par. No, these will do.
  Ing. Tell me now about your home—I will sit here
Near thee.
  Par. Not there: thou art crushing all the flowers.
  Ing. (*Seating himself at her feet.*)
Well, well; I will sit here, then. And now tell me,
What is your name!
  Par.   Parthenia.
  Ing.   Parthenia!
A pretty name! and now, Parthenia, tell me
How that which you call love grows in the soul;
And what love is: 'tis strange, but in that word [less
There's something seems like yonder ocean—fathom-
  Par. How shall I say? Love comes, my mother
    says,
Like flowers in the night—reach me those violets——
It is a flame a single look will kindle,
But not an ocean quench.
Fostered by dreams, excited by each thought,
Love is a star from heaven, that points the way
And leads us to its home—a little spot
In earth's dry desert, where the soul may rest—
A grain of gold in the dull sand of life—
A foretaste of Elysium; but when,
Weary of this world's woes, the immortal gods
Flew to the skies, with all their richest gifts,

Love stayed behind, self-exiled for man's sake!
Ing. I never yet heard aught so beautiful!
But still I comprehend it not.
Par.   Nor I.
For I have never felt it; yet I know
A song my mother sang, an ancient song,
That plainly speaks of love at least to me.
How goes it? stay—

> [*Slowly, as trying to recollect.*

> 'What love is, if thou wouldst be taught,
>   Thy heart must teach alone,—
> Two souls with but a single thought,
>   Two hearts that beat as one.'

> 'And whence comes love? like morning's light,
>   It comes without thy call;
> And how dies love?—A spirit bright,
>   Love never dies at all!'

And when—and when——

> [*Hesitating as unable to continue.*

Ing. Go on.
Par. I know no more.
Ing. (*Impatiently.*) Try—Try.
Par. I cannot now; but at some other time
I may remember.
Ing. (*Somewhat authoritatively.*) Now, go on I say.
Par. (*Springing up in alarm.*)   Not now, I want
    more roses for my wreath!
Yonder they grow, I will fetch them for myself.
Take care of all my flowers and the wreath! [*runs off.*

> [*Throws the flowers into Ingomar's lap and*
Ing. (*after a pause, without changing his position,*
    speaking to himself in deep abstraction.)

> 'Two souls with but a single thought,
>   Two hearts that beat as one.'

MARGARET.

O sweet pale Margaret,
O rare pale Margaret,
What lit your eyes with tearful power,
Like moonlight on a falling shower?
Who lent you, love, your mortal dower
  Of pensive thought and aspect pale,
  Your melancholy sweet and frail
As perfume of the cuckoo-flower?
From the westward winding flood,
From the evening-lighted wood,
  From all things outward you have won
A tearful grace, as though you stood
  Between the rainbow and the sun.
The very smile before you speak,
That dimples your transparent cheek,
  Encircles all the heart, and feedeth
The senses with a still delight
  Of dainty sorrow without sound,
  Like the tender amber round,
 Which the moon around her spreadeth,
Moving through a fleecy night.

You love, remaining peaceful,
  To hear the murmur of the strife
  But enter not the toil of life.
Your spirit is the calméd sea,
  Laid by the tumult of the fight.
You are the evening star, alway
  Remaining betwixt dark and bright :
Lull'd echoes of laborious day
  Come to you, gleams of mellow light
 . Float by you on the verge of night.
What can it matter, Margaret,
  What songs below the waning stars,
The lion-heart, Plantagenet,

Sang, looking through his prison bars?
Exquisite Margaret, who can tell
The last wild thought of Chatelet,
Just ere the falling axe did part
The burning brain from the true heart,
Even in her sight he loved so well?

A fairy shield your Genius made,
And gave you on your natal day.
Your sorrow, only sorrow's shade,
Keeps real sorrow far away.
You move not in such solitudes,
You are not less divine,
But more human in your moods,
Than your twin-sister, Adeline,
Your hair is darker, and your eyes
Touched with a somewhat darker hue,
And less aërially blue,
But ever trembling through the dew
Of dainty-woful sympathies.

O sweet pale Margaret,
O rare pale Margaret,
Come down, come down, and hear me speak:
Tie up the ringlets on your cheek:
The sun is just about to set,
The arching lines are tall and shady,
And faint, rainy lights are seen,
Moving in the heavy beech.
Rise from the feast of sorrow, lady,
Where all day long you sit between
Joy and woe, and whisper each.
Or only look across the lawn,
Look out below your bower eaves,
Look down, and let your blue eyes dawn
Upon me through the jasmine leaves.

MY HUSBAND.

A surging crowd, a woman's piteous cry,
  A mocking laugh and lightly uttered jest,
Are all that reach me as they hurry by.
  But the full meaning I have rightly guessed—
Another tenant for the prison cell,
  A woman, too! the pity of it all!
What has she done? Alas! I cannot tell;
  They'll tell me later when I chance to call.

    *   *   *   *   *   *

I find the woman sitting in her cell,
  Wringing her hands, and shedding bitter tears,
Her thin, pale cheeks their tale of sorrow tell;
  Her bony form, too, bent, but not with years.
Her eyes meet mine, but ere my tongue can speak
  She falls upon her knees upon the floor,
Crying, "Oh! God forgive me, I was weak;
  But he will die, and I could beg no more.

"Why have you torn me from him? Let me go!
  You will not leave him there to die alone,
While I, his lawful wife, am here? Oh! no:
  Let me go to him, if you are not stone.
I tell you he is dying, sir, for bread—
  A big strong man, sir, murdered in his prime!
I could not beg the food; I stole instead; ·
  Stole, sir, to save his life! Was that a crime?

"For fifteen years we've labored side by side;
  For fifteen years his faithful wife I've been;
And many a time, sir, we've been sorely tried,
  For many a bitter trouble we have seen.
Our children died of hunger, one by one;
  We could not feed them as they should be fed.
They died! We tried to say, 'Thy will be done,'
  But 'tisn't easy when your hopes are dead.

"And many a time we said we'd have no more,
  But when we saw some neighbor's baby-boy,

And watched his childish gambols round our door,
　　And marked the mother's pride, the father's joy—
Why, we were human, sir, and thought, alas!
　　That Heaven perchance might let the next one stay
But one by one they withered like the grass,
　　And one by one they died and passed away.

"And all the years we've struggled, he and I,
　　To keep our sorrows hid from mortal eyes.
'Cheer up, dear, things will brighten by and by ;
　　The world is hard but God is good and wise.'
That's what he always said when things went wrong,
　　When work was scarce, and food was hard to get—
'Cheer up, dear, he would say ; 'it won't be long ;
　　Let's trust in God, He's never failed us yet !'

"And we have waited—sometimes waited long—
　　And we have prayed for help, and help has come.
But every winter something has gone wrong,
　　And every year we've been without a home.
The little treasures we would fain have kept—
　　The playthings of our dear ones dead and gone—
Were sold for food ! How bitterly we wept,
　　They only guess who such a grief have known.

"And then this illness came and struck him down.
　　And he grew weak and weaker every day ;
While I have done odd jobs about the town
　　To earn him food, and help and pay the way.
But he grew worse ! And then the doctor came,
　　And ordered med'cine, nourishment, and wine.
Oh ! he meant well, sir ; he was not to blame ;
　　He did his duty—and then I did mine !

"For two days I had neither bite nor sup.
　　Oh ! how I suffered ; but he never knew.
And every hour more bitter grew my cup,
　　For every hour still worse and worse he grew.
Then work ran short. I begged, and begged in vain.
　　'Cheer up my lass,' he said, 'the times will mend !

We've trusted God before; let's trust again;
We need not fear while we have such a friend!'

"But every day the fiercer grew our need,
And hunger gnawed us like a savage beast.
My frenzied brain conceived the desperate deed [least.
Of theft! Was't crime? 'Twould save his life at
God knows that I could see no other way.
Had I not begged and prayed—and both in vain?
I did not think of what the world might say—
If that would save him, I could bear the stain!

"I stood outside a fashionable shop,
And watched the tide of wealth go rolling in;
And as I gazed, I saw a carriage stop—
My soul burned with the fever of my sin!
A lady stepped out, clad in silks so grand,
And holding in her dainty clasp a purse;
I darted forward, snatched it from her hand
And fled, like one who flees before a curse.

"But I was weak and faint, and swifter feet
Than mine were following, and soon ran me down.
Policemen came and dragged me through the street;
And I am now the by-word of the town.
And he is dying there, while I am here,
And cannot soothe or raise his fevered head.
For God's sake, take me to him! Never fear,
I'll come back here again—when he is dead!

"Do with me what you will when he is gone;
I care not then what punishment you give.
But do not let him perish there alone;
Do with me what you will, but let him live!
Oh! save his life, sir, and I'll be your slave,
And God will send His blessings on your head.
Don't let them put him in a pauper's grave,
And treat him like dog when he is dead!

"God bless you, sir! Oh! speak those words again!
 You'll take me out? Oh! quick, then ; let us go.
Thank Heaven, this time I have not begged in vain.
 Why don't they let us out? They are so slow. . .
Don't tell him I've been here, sir; he is ill!
 Poor dear, he never had a thought of wrong.
Don't let him know this, sir ; the shame would kill.
 He always said, 'Wait, dear, it won't be long.'

  * * * * * *

"Ah! here it is, sir; mind the broken stair.
 It's dark, sir; for we can't afford a light.
We're glad to find a shelter anywhere ;
 It's hard to walk about the streets all night.
Ah! there he is! John, dear, I've come again ;
 I'm sorry, dear, you've had so long to wait.
What's this?—He's cold!—Oh! I have come in vain—
 He's dead! He's dead! And I am too late, too late!

  * * * * * *

And as this happened in a Christian land?
 It comes before me like a hideous dream.
Too true, alas! I hear on every hand
 The orphan's wail, the widow's anguished scream.
And poverty, red-eyed, stalks gaunt and bare,
 While pampered Wealth sits in the justice seat!
But hark! a sentence cleaves the humid air—
 'They hungered and ye gave them not to eat!'"

HAWKINS.

ROUND THE BIVOUAC FIRE.

Round the bivouac fire, at midnight,
 Lay the weary warrior-band;
Bloody were their spears with slaughter ;
 Gory was each hero's hand:
For the ghastly fight was ended:
 From each soul a whisper came:
"God of Battles! we have triumphed:
 Hallowed be Thy mighty Name!"

It was beautiful, at midnight,
  When the bloody war was done,
When the battle clashed no longer,
  And no longer blazed the sun,
Calmly, in the balmy starlight,
  To repose our wearied limbs,
Not a sound to stir the stillness,
  Save the sound of holy hymns;

"Thou hast given us the glory:
  Thou hast cast our foes to shame!
God of Battles we have triumphed;
  Hallowed be Thy mighty Name!
Thou hast given us the glory:
  Thou hast bade our troubles cease:
Thou art great as God of Battles:
  Thou art best as God of Peace!"

Peaceful was the world around them:
  In the peaceful summer skies
Watched the sentry stars above them,
  Like the host of angel-eyes:
Shone the sentinel stars in splendour
  On each slumbering hero's head,
And the moonlight gleamed in glory
  On the dying and the dead.

Rosily wore the night to morning:
  Cheerily, at their heart's desire,
Sang the soldiers songs of triumph,
  Round the ruddy bivouac fire:
Flushed their faces were with glory:
  Strong were they, and brave, and tall:
But the tender tears of childhood
  Bathed the bravest face of all!

Pensive, by the gleaming firelight,
  Mute the lonely warrior stood:
In his hand a paper grasped he,
  Scrawled with letters, large and crude:
In his gory hands he grasped it;
  And the tender childly tear,

From his manly bosom welling,
  Bathed the blood upon his spear!

Silent wore the night to morning:
  Silent, at their heart's desire,
Watching, lay the weary warriors,
  Round the gleaming bivouac fire:
What's the news from home, dear comrade?
  What's the sorry news for thee,
From the friends we left behind us,
  And our home beyond the sea?"

Then the gory paper oped he,
  Scrawled with letters, crude and wild:
"Little news from home, dear comrades:
  'Tis a letter from my child.'
"From our merry merry babes,
  Welcome is the news!" they said:
And the soldiers lay in silence,
  While the warrior rose, and read:

"Oh my father! what has kept you?
  You are nigh three years away:
It was snow-time when you left us:
  It was morn o' New Year's day;
'Good-by, baby, until summer,
  Or till Christmas time,' you said:
Oh my father! what has kept you?
  Summer, Christmas, twice have fled.

"Mother says our war is holy—
  That you bear a noble name—
That you fight for God and Honor,
  And to shield our home from shame;
But I often hear her praying:
  'Make all war, O God to cease:
Thou art great as God of battles:
  Thou art best as God of Peace!'

"Night and morn I pray for father:
  In the sunny morning hours
I am often in the garden:
  I have sown your name in flowers!

Like your coat, in flowers of scarlet—
   All in tulips, soldier-red;
Come, before the flowers are faded:
   Come before your name is dead!

" Little brother died at Christmas:
   Mother told me not to tell:
But I think it better, father;
   For you said, 'The dead are well.'
He was buried side o' Mary:
   Mother since has never smiled:
Till we meet, good-by, dear father—
   From your little loving child! "

Silent wore the night to morning:
   Silent, at their soul's desire,
Lay the warriors, lost in dreaming,
   Round the dying bivouac fire:
Home were they, once more, once more!
   Miles were they from war's alarms!
Hark! the sudden bugle sounding!
   Hark! the cry: "To arms! to arms! "

Out from ambush, out from thicket,
   Charged the foemen through the plain!
"Up! my warriors! arm! my heroes!
   Strike for God and home again!
For our homes, our babes, our country! "
   And the ruddy morning light
Flared on brandished falchions bloody
   Still with gore of yesternight!

Purple grew the plain with slaughter—
   Steed and rider, side by side;
And the crimson day of carnage
   In a crimson sunset died:
Shuddering on the field of battle
   Glimpsed the starlight overhead,
And the moon-light, ghost-like,
   Glimmered on the dying and the dead!

Faint and few, around the fire-light,
  Were the stretched, outwearied limbs :
Faint and few the hero-voices
  That uprose in holy hymns:
Few the warriors left to whisper,
  "Thou hast cast our foes to shame :
God of battles we have triumphed :
  Hallowed be thy mighty Name!"

On the purple plain of slaughter,
  Who is this that smiles in rest,
With a shred of gory paper
  Lying on his mangled breast?
Nought remaining, save a fragment,
  Scrawled with letters, crude and wild:
"Till we meet, good-by, dear father—
  From your little loving child!"

Raise him softly; lift him gently:
  Stanch his life-blood, ebbing slow:
He is breathing—he is whispering—
  What is this he murmurs low?
"Saved! my child—my home—my country!
  Father, give my pangs release:
Thou art great as God of Battles :
  Thou art best as God of Peace!"

THE CRY OF THE POOR.

The heart of the City is black with sin,
  Black in its inmost core ;
For Sorrow, God's shadow, falls dark within
  The hopeless homes of the poor;
The strong man gnaweth his iron chain,
  And hungers from night to morn,
The woman lying apart in pain
  Curses the babe unborn ;
The little children make moan alway,
  Shelterless, starven, bereaven,

With souls that glimmer thro' slender clay,
　And beacon their mothers from heaven.
　　The rich man's larder is richly stored,
　　　But the poor look up unfed;
　　The rich man cries, "Give us light, O Lord!"
　　　The hungry, "Give us bread!"

Blackness from morn till the pitiless stars
　Veil their religion of light,
And blackness too when the brazen bars
　Of sunset are molten in night;
Blackness of alley, and street, and lane,
　Where singeth never a bird;
And yet in the midst of the pang and pain
　No prayer for the light is heard:
The starving and destitute would not know:
　Their spirits unclean and stark,
Circumscribed by their need and their woe,
　Are better they say, in the dark.
　　The rich man seeketh a pleasant sky
　　　Beyond the graves of the dead;
　　And "Lord give us light!" the wealthy cry,
　　　The hungry, "Give us bread!"

The rich man hoardeth his nobler woe
　To savor his pleasure and love;
The sweet delight of his earth below
　Doth color his heaven above;
His hopes lie beautiful on before,
　He knoweth no petty strife,
And he has raiment and food in store
　For his little ones and wife;
He craveth for light, while overhead
　He perceives the golden day;
In flowery pleasures his babes are led,
　And he has leisure to pray.
　　The rich man worshipping God by night,
　　　Sees the beckoning stars overhead;
　　The rich man prayeth, "Lord, give me light!"
　　　The hungry give me bread!"

The poor man hungereth in his doubt,
  He can see nor stars nor sky,
For his eyes are on earth as he hollows out
  Graves for the loved as they die ;
He struggles onward in troublous breath,
  With no holy of holies above,
Subtracting the wormwood of life and death
  From the pity of God and His love ;
The dead and buried are not to him
  Sweet charters to conquer the tomb,—
They gleam like angry devils and dim
  On the brink of a fathomless gloom.
    The rich man's earthier paradise
    Hints a heaven beyond the dead ;
      And "Lord, give us light!" the rich man cries,
      The hungry, "Give us bread!"

"Bread, give us bread!" the poor man says;
  "Bread, bread!" cry children and wives;
And "Lord, give us light!" the rich man prays,
  The light of Thy holier lives.
The cries clash daily without accord,
  They cease not morning or night,
The wealthy ask not for bread, O Lord,
  The starving ask not for light;
There cometh no rest to low or to high,
  Woe mirroreth earth, joy, heaven;
The poor ask bread, and the wealthy try
  To sweeten the bread which is given.
    The rich man, master of earth, seeks more
    Beyond the graves of the dead ;
      But, narrow'd to that they lack, the poor
      Cry loudly, "Give us bread!"

Ah, me!—to wander with ears and eyes,
  Thro' alley, and street, and lane,
To see the visions of paradise
  Obscured by the grosser pain ;
To see the strong man shrink from the path
  That leadeth up to the sky.

To see the hungry arise in wrath,
    And deny the light, and die;—
Oh, heal the earthly bitterness first,
    Sisters and brothers mine;
And after bread should follow the thirst
    For the light which is divine!
        The rich man's plentiful nights and days
            Are radiant with pleasures fled;
        And "Lord give us light!" the rich man prays,
            The hungry, "Give me bread!"

Out in the fields where the sun is bright,
    Upspringeth the yellow corn,
It springs and grows in the shining light
    Till the bountiful acres are shorn;
The reaper reapeth on golden ground,
    And the sun-tanned gleaners glean,
And the wheels of the mill go busily round
    With the rich white grain between.
But the hungry live in the crowded street,
    In poverty, sickness and pain—
'Tis the blessèd and bountiful grain they entreat,
    Not the light that has ripened the grain!
    *   *   *   *   *

And toiling downward, the homeless poor
    Seek graves as their only goals;
The draught that comes from the rich man's door
    Blows out the lamps of their souls;
And reft of the guarding and guiding light
    The beautiful Soul must give,
They hunger on in the pitiless night,
    Knowing only by need that they live;
And stretched apart as the dregs of life,
    They rot on the rich man's land,
And when death cometh for baby or wife
    They gnaw at his outstretched hand!
        They ask not light to reveal the hate
            In the eyes of living and dead:
        "Light!" cry the wealthy early and late,
            The poor ask only for bread!

                                        BUCHANNAN.

THE COUNTESS AND THE SERF.

LOVE.——Act I.—Scene 2.

Countess. Give o'er! I hate the poet's argument!
'Tis falsehood—'tis offence.   A noble maid
Stoop to a peasant!—Ancestry, sire, dam,
Kindred, and all, of perfect blood, despised
For love!
 Huon. The peasant, though of humble stock,
High nature did enoble—
 Coun. What was that?
Mean you to justify it?   But go on.
 Huon. Not to offend.   [*Rises and comes forward.*
 Coun. Offend!—No fear of that,
I hope, 'twixt thee and me!   I pray you, sir,
To recollect yourself and be at ease,
And as I bid you, do.   Go on.
 Huon. Descent,
You'll grant, is not alone nobility,
Will you not?   Never yet was line so long,
But it beginning had; and that was found
In rarity of nature, giving one
Advantage over many; aptitude
For arms, for counsel, so superlative
As baffled all competitors, and made
The many glad to follow him as guide
Or safeguard.
Not in descent alone, then, lies degree,
Which from descent to nature may be traced,
Its proper fount?   And that, which nature did,
You'll grant she may be like to do again;
And in a very peasant, yea, a slave,
Enlodge the worth that roots the noble tree.
      [*The* Countess *eyes him.*
I trust I seem not bold, to argue so.
 Coun. Sir, when to me it matters what you seem,
Make question on't.   If you have more to say,
Proceed—yet mark you how the poet mocks
Himself the advocacy; in the sequel

His hero is a hind in masquerade!
He proves to be a lord.
　Huon. The poet sinned
Against himself, in that! He should have known
A better trick, who had at hand his own
Excelling nature to admonish him,
Than the low cunning of the common craft,
A hind, his hero, won the lady's love:
He had worth enough for that! Her heart was his.
Wedlock joins nothing, if it joins not hearts.
Marriage was never meant for coats of arms.
Heraldry flourishes on metal, silk,
Or wood.　Examine as you will the blood,
No painting on't is there?—as red, as warm,
The peasant's as the noble's!
　Coun. Dost thou know
Thou speak'st to me?
　Huon. 'Tis therefore so I speak.
　Coun. And know'st thy duty to me?
　Huon. Yes.
　Coun. And see'st
My station, and thy own?
　Huon. I see my own.
　Coun. Not mine?
　Huon. I cannot, for the fair
O'ertopping height before.
　Coun. What height?
　Huon. Thyself,
That towerest 'bove thy station!—Pardon me!
Oh, would'st thou set thy rank before thyself?
Wouldst thou be honored for thyself, or that?
Rank that excels its wearer, doth degrade ;
Riches impoverish, that divide respect.
　.　.　　Kings from their thrones cast down,
Have blessed their fate, that they were valued for
Themselves, and not their stations, when some knee,
That hardly bowed to them in plenitude,
Has kissed the dust before them, stripped of all! [this,
　Coun. [*Confused.*] I nothing see that's relative in

That bears upon the argument.
    Huon. Oh, much,
Durst but my heart explain.
    Coun. Has thou a heart?
I thought thou wast a serf; and, as a serf,
Had'st thought and will none other than thy lord's,
And so no heart—that is, no heart of thine own.
But since thou say'st thou hast a heart, 'tis well,—
Keep it a secret; let me not suspect   [*smiles.*
What, were it e'en suspicion, were thy death.   [Huon
Sir, did I name a banquet to thee now,
Thou lookedst so?
    Huon. To die for thee were such.
    Coun. Sir?
    Huon. For his master oft a serf has died,
And thought it sweet; and may not, then, a serf
Say, for his mistress 'twere a feast to die?
    Coun. Thou art presumptuous—very—so, no wonder
If I misunderstood thee. Thou'dst do well
To be thyself, and nothing more.
    Huon. Myself!   [thou
    Coun. Why, art thou not a serf? What right hast
To set thy person off with such a bearing?
And move with such a gait? to give thy brow .
The set of nobles, and thy tongue his phrase?
Thy betters' clothes sit fairer upon thee
Than on themselves, "and they were made for them.'
I have no patience with thee—can't abide thee!
There are no bounds to thy ambition, none!
How durst thou e'er adventure to bestride
The war-horse—sitting him, that people say
Thou, not the knight, appear'st his proper load?
How durst thou touch the lance, the battle-axe,
And wheel the flaming falchion round thy head,
As thou would'st blaze the son of chivalry?
I know! my father found thy aptitude,
And humored it, to boast thee off! He may chance
To rue it; and no wonder if he should,
If others' eyes see that they should not see,

Shown to them by his own.

Huon. Oh, lady—

Coun. What?

Huon. Heard I aright?

Coun. Aright—what heard'st thou, then?
I would not think thee so presumptuous
As through thy pride to misinterpret me.
It were not for thy health,—yea, for thy life!
Beware, sir. It would not set my quiet blood,
On haste for mischief to thee, rushing through
My veins, did I believe!—Thou art not mad;
Knowing thy vanity, I aggravate it.
Thou know'st 'twere shame, the lowest free-woman
That follows in my train should think of thee!

Huon. I know it, lady.

Coun. That I meant to say,
No more. Don't read such books to me again.
I would you had not learned to read so well,
I had been spared your annotations.
For the future, no reply, when I remark,
Hear, but don't speak—unless you're told—and then
No more than you are told; what makes the answer up,
No syllable beyond.   [Huon *retires up*, C.

Enter Falconer *with hawk*, R.

My Falconer! So.   [*Crosses*, L.
An hour I'll fly my hawk.

Falconer. A noble bird,
My lady, knows his bells, is proud of them.

Coun. They are no portion of his excellence:
It is his own! 'Tis not by them he makes
His ample wheel; mounts up, and up, and up,
In spiry rings, piercing the firmament,
Till he o'ertops his prey; then gives his stoop,
More fleet and sure than ever arrow sped!
How nature fashioned him for his bold trade
Gave him his stars of eyes to range abroad,
His wings of glorious spread to mow the air,
And breast of might to use them! I delight
To fly my hawk. The hawk's a glorious bird;
You may be useful, sir; wait upon me.
Obedient—yet a daring, dauntless bird!   KNOWLES.

THE IDIOT LAD.

The vesper hymn had died away.
    And the benison had been said,
But one remained in church to pray,
    With a bow'd and reverent head.
He could not frame in words the prayer
    Which reached the Throne of Grace,
But the Love and Pity present there
    Saw the pleading of his face.

In many curls hung his hair of gold,
    Round a brow of pearly white;
His face was cast in a graceful mould,
    And his eyes were strangely bright.
Gentle his white hand's touch—his smile
    Was tender and sweet and sad,
Nought knew the whole of fraud and guile
    Of poor Dick, the idiot lad,

"My boy," I said, "the tired sun
    Sinks low on the west sea's breast;
The shades which fall when the day is done
    Woo the weary earth to rest.
In the vesper zephyr's gentle stir
    The sleepy tree-tops nod—
Why wait you here?" and he said, "Oh, sir,
    I would see the face of God!

"If the sun is so fair in his noon-day pride,
    And the moon in the silver night;
If the stars which by angels at eventide
    Are lighted can shine so bright!
If wood and dell, each flow'r and tree,
    And each grass of the graveyard sod,
Are so full of beauty, oh, what must it be
    To look on the Face of God.

"I have sought for the vision wide and near,
    And once, sir, I travell'd far
To a mighty city long leagues from here,

Where men of the great world are.
But the faces I saw were false and mean,
    And cruel, and hard, and bad;
And none like the Face the saints have seen
    Saw poor Dick, the idiot lad.

"In the night, sir, I wander away from home;
    Down the lanes and the fields I go—
Thro' the silent and lonely woods I roam,
    Patient, and praying, and slow.
In the early morn on the hills I stand,
    Ere yet the mists have past;
And I eagerly look o'er sea and land
    For the wonderful vision at last.

"When the lightning's flash and the thunders roar,
    And the ships fly in from the gale;
When the waves beat high on the shrinking shore,
    And the fishing boats dare not sail;
I seek it still, in the storm and snow,
    Lest it may happen to be,
That then it will please the great God to show
    His beautiful Face to me.

"I seek it still when God's gleaming pledge
    In the bright'ning sky appears,
And from tree and flower, and sparkling hedge
    Earth is weeping her happy tears;
For I sometimes think that I may behold,
    After yearning years of pain,
The Face of my God in the quivering gold
    Of the sunshine that follows rain.

"When the fishers return on the homeward tide,
    I ask them nothing but this:
'Have you seen it out there on the ocean wide,
    Where the sky and the water kiss?'
But they smile, and 'Poor Dick' I hear them say,
    And they answer me always 'No.'
So I think I must be still farther away
    Then even the fishing boats go."

That night while the simple fisher-folk slept,
  From the dreams of the mighty free,
Down to the beach the Idiot crept,
  And launched on the summer sea.
And the boat sped on, and on, and on,
  From the ever-receding shore,
And brighter and brighter the moonbeams shone,
  Which for him were to shine no more.

Far out at sea his boat was found,
  And the tide, which bore to land
The village fleet from the fishing ground,
  Laid softly upon the sand
The white wet face of the idiot boy,
  Not yearning and wistful now,
For perfect peace, and rest, and joy
  Were written upon his brow.

In the poor lad's eyes seem'd still the glow
  Of a new and wondrous light:
And down on the beach the women knelt low
  As they gaz'd on the holy sight.
As the fishermen walk'd to the smiling dead,
  Softly their rough feet trod;
And bared was each head, as one slowly said,
  "He was look'd on the Face of God!"

OVERTON.

THE LOVERS.

THE LADY OF LYONS.——Act II.—Scene 1.

Melnotte. You can be proud of your connection
with one who owes his position to merit,—not birth.
Pauline. Why, yes; but still——
Mel. Still what, Pauline?
Pauline. There is something glorious in the Herit-

age of Command. A man who has ancestors is like a Representative of the Past.

Mel. True; but,like other representatives, nine times out of ten he is a silent member. Ah, Pauline! not to the Past, but to the Future, looks true nobility, and finds its blazon in posterity.   [*Leading her to seat,* R. C.

Pauline. You say this to please me, who have no ancestors; but you, Prince, must be proud of so illustrious a race!

Mel. No, no! I would not, were I fifty times a prince, be a pensioner on the Dead. I honor birth and ancestry when they are regarded as the incentives to exertion not the title-deeds to sloth; I honor the laurels that overshadow the graves of our fathers;—it is our fathers I emulate, when I desire that beneath the evergreen I myself have planted my own ashes may repose! Dearest, could'st thou but see with my eyes!

Pauline. I cannot forego pride when I look on thee and think that thou lovest me. (*Rises.*) Sweet Prince, tell me again of thy palace by the Lake of Como; it is so pleasant to hear of thy splendor since thou didst swear to me that they would be desolate without Pauline; and when thou describest them, it is with a mocking lip and a noble scorn, as if custom had made thee disdain greatness.   [paint

Mel. Nay, dearest, nay, if thou would'st have me
The home to which, could Love fulfil its prayers,
This hand would lead thee, listen!—A deep vale
Shut out by Alpine hills from the rude world;
Near a clear lake, margin'd by fruits of gold
And whispering myrtles; glassing softest skies
As cloudless, save with rare and roseate shadows,
As I would have thy fate!

Pauline. My own dear love!

Mel. A palace lifting to eternal summer
Its marble walls, from out a glossy bower
Of coolest foliage musical with birds,
Whose songs should syllable thy name! At noon
We'd sit beneath the arching vines, and wonder
Why Earth could be unhappy, while the Heavens

Still left us youth and love!   We'd have no friends
That were not lovers; no ambition, save
To excel them all in love; we'd read no books
That were not tales of love—that we might smile
To think how poorly eloquence of words
Translates the poetry of hearts like ours!
And when night came, amidst the breathless Heavens
We'd guess what star should be our home when love
Becomes immortal; while the perfumed light
Stole through the mists of alabaster lamps,
And every air was heavy with the sighs
Of orange-groves and music from sweet lutes,
And murmurs of low fountains that gush forth
I' the midst of roses!—Dost thou like the picture?
     Pauline. Oh, as the bee upon the flower, I hang
Upon the honey of thy eloquent tongue!
Am I not blest? And if I love too wildly,
Who would not love thee like Pauline?
     Mel. (*Bitterly.*) Oh, false one!
It is the *prince* thou lovest, not the *man ;*
If in the stead of luxury, and pomp, and power,
I had painted poverty, toil, and care,
Thou hadst found no honey on my tongue;—Pauline,
That is not love.   (*Crosses to* R.)
     Pauline. Thou wrong'st me, cruel Prince!
At first, in truth, I might not have been won,
Save through the weakness of a flattered pride;
But *now*,—oh! trust me,—could'st thou fall from power
And sink——
     Mel. As low as that poor gardener's son
Who dared to lift his eyes to thee?
     Pauline. Even then,
Methinks thou would'st be only made more dear
By the sweet thought that I could prove how deep
Is woman's love!   We are like the insects, caught
By the glittering of a garish flame;
But, oh, the wings once scorch'd, the brightest star
Lures us no more; and by the fatal light
We cling till death!

TWO WOMEN.

A grandma sits in her great armchair;
  Balmy sweet is the soft spring air.
Through the latticed, lilac-shadowed pane
  She looks to the orchard beyond the lane;
And she catches the gleam of a woman's dress,
  As it flutters about in the wind's caress.
"That child is glad as the day is long—
  Her lover is coming, her life's a song!"
Up from the orchard's flowery bloom
  Floats fragrance faint to the darkening room
Where grandma dreams, till a tender grace
  And a softer light steals into her face.
For once again she is young and fair,
  And twining roses in her hair.
Once again, blithe as the lark above.
  She is only a girl, and a girl in love!
The years drop from her their weary pain;
  She is clasped in her lover's arms again!
The last faint glimmers of daylight die;
  Stars tremble out of the purple sky;
Ere Dora flits up the garden path,
  Sadly afraid of grandma's wrath.
With rose-red cheeks and flying hair,
  She nestles down by the old armchair.
"Grandma, Dick says, may we—may—I—"
  The faltering voice grows strangely shy;
But Grandma presses the little hand:
  "Yes, my dearie, I understand!
"He may have you, darling!" Not all in vain
  Did grandma dream she was young again!
She gently twists a shining curl;
  Ah, me! the philosophy of a girl!
Take the world's treasures—its noblest, best—
  And love will outweigh all the rest!
And through the casement the moonlight cold
  Streams on two heads—one gray, one gold.

THE SUNRISE NEVER FAILED US YET.

Upon the sadness of the sea,
The sunset broods regretfully;
From the far lonely spaces slow
Withdraws the wistful after-glow
So out of life the splendor dies,
So darken all the happy skies,
So gathers twilight, cold and stern,
But overhead the planets burn.
And up the east another day,
Shall chase the bitter dawn away:
What though our eyes with tears be wet!
The sunrise never failed us yet.
The blush of dawn may yet restore
Our light, and hope, and joy once more;
Sad soul, take comfort, nor forget
That sunrise never failed us yet.

CELIA THAXTER.

THE NEGLECTED CHILD.

I never was a favorite—
    My mother never smiled
On me, with half the tenderness
    That blessed her fairer child.
I've seen her kiss my sister's cheek,
    While fondled on her knee;
I've turned away to hide my tears, —
    There was no kiss for me!

And yet I strove to please with all
    My little store of sense;
I strove to please, and infancy
    Can rarely give offence.
But when my artless efforts met
    A cold, ungentle check,
I did not dare to throw myself,
    In tears, upon her neck.

How blessèd are the beautiful!
    Love watches o'er their birth;
Oh! beauty in my nursery

I learned to know thy worth :—
For even there, I often felt
Forsaken and forlorn, .
And wished—for others wished it too—
I never had been born!

I'm sure I was affectionate,—
But in my sister's face,
There was a look of love that claimed
A smile, or an embrace.
But when I raised my lip, to meet
The pressure children prize,
None knew the feelings of my heart,—
They spoke not in my eyes.

But oh! that heart too keenly felt
The anguish of neglect;
I saw my sister's lovely form
With gems and roses decked;
I did not covet them; but oft,
When wantonly reproved,
I envied her the privilege
Of being so beloved.

But soon a time of triumph came—
A time of sorrow too,—
For sickness o'er my sister's form
Her venomed mantle threw:—
The features, once so beautiful,
Now wore the hue of death;
And former friends shrank fearfully
From her infectious breath.

'Twas then, unwearied, day and night
I watched beside her bed,
And fearlessly upon my breast
I pillowed her poor head.
She lived!—she loved me for my care!
My grief was at an end;
I was a lonely being once,
But now I have a friend.

RED RIDING HOOD.

On the wide lawn the snow lay deep,
Ridged o'er with many a drifted heap,
The wind that through the pine trees sung
The naked elm boughs tossed and swung;
While through the window, frosty-starred,
Against the sunset purple barred,
We saw the sombre crow flap by,
The hawk's grey fleck along the sky,
The crested blue-jay flitting swift,
Erect, alert, his thick grey tail
Set to the north wind like a sail.

It came to pass our little lass,
With flattened face against the glass,
And eyes in which the tender dew
Of pity shone, stood gazing through
The narrow space her rosy lips
Had melted from the frost's eclipse ;
"Oh, see," she cried, "the poor blue-jays !
What is that the black crow says ?
The squirrel lifts his little legs
Because he has no hands, and begs ;
He's asking for my nuts, I know ;
May I not feed them on the snow ?"

Half lost within her boots, her head
Warm sheltered in her hood of red,
Her plaid skirt close about her drawn,
She floundered down the wintry lawn ;
Now struggling through the misty vail
Blown round her by the shrieking gale ;
Now sinking in a drift so low
Her scarlet hood could scarcely show
Its dash of color on the snow.
She dropped for bird and beast forlorn
Her little store of nuts and corn,
And thus her timid guests bespoke :
"Come, squirrel, from yon hollow oak—

Come, black old crow—come, poor blue-jay,
Before your supper is blown away!
Don't be afraid; we all are good;
And I'm mamma's Red Riding Hood!"

O Thou whose care is over all,
Who heedest e'en the sparrow's fall,
Keep in the little maiden's breast
The pity which is now its guest!
Let not her cultured years make less
The childhood charm of tenderness,
But let her feel as well as now,
Nor harder with her polish grow!
Unmoved by sentimental grief
That wails along some printed leaf,
But prompt with kindly word and deed
To own the claims of all who need,
Let the grown woman's self make good
The promise of Red Riding Hood!

WHITTIER.

THE ROMAN MAIDEN IN LOVE.

VIRGINIUS.——Act I.—Scene 2.

Virginia. How is it with my heart? I feel as one
That has lost every thing, and just before
Had nothing left to wish for! He will cast
Icilius off!—I never told it yet;
But take of me, thou gentle air, the secret—
And ever after breathe more balmy sweet—
I love Icilius! Yes, I love Icilius!
My father'll cast him off!—not if Icilius
Approve his honor. That he'll ever do;
He speaks, and looks, and moves, a thing of honor,
Or honor never yet spoke, look'd or mov'd,
Or was a thing on earth. O, come, Icilius;
Do but appear, and thou art vindicated.
        [*Enter* Icilius, *and takes her hand.*
  Icilius. Virginia! my Virginia! I am all
Dissolv'd—o'erpower'd with the munificence

Of this auspicious hour. I love thee, but
To make thee happy! If to make thee so
Be bliss denied to me—lo, I release
The gifted hand—that I would faster hold,
Than wretches, bound for death, would cling to life—
If thou would'st take it back—then take it back.
 Virginia. I take it back—to give thee again!
 Icil. O help me to a word will speak my bliss,
Or I am beggar'd—No! there is not one!
There cannot be; for never man had bliss,
Like mine to name.
 Virg. I'd help thee to
A hundred words; each one of which would far
O'er-rate thy gain, and yet no single one
Rate over high!
 Icil. Thou could'st not do it! No;
Pick from each rarer pattern of thy sex
Her rarest charm, till thou hast every charm
Of soul and body, that can blend in woman,
I would out-paragon the paragon
With thee. No! I will not let thee win,
On such a theme as this!
 Virg. Nor will I drop
The controversy, that the richer makes me
The more I lose.
 Icil. My sweet Virginia.
We do but lose and lose, and win and win;
"Playing for nothing but lose and win;"   *her.*
Then tell us stop the game: and thus I stop it. [*Kisses*

KNOWLES.

TO MARY.

There are some who may shine as thee, Mary!
And many more frank and free,
And a few as fair;
But the summer air
Is not more sweet to me, Mary!

CORNWALL.

RECALLED BY A TOUCH.

I met her, she was thin and cold;
  She stooped, and trod with tottering feet:
The hair was gray that once was gold,
  The voice was harsh that once was sweet
Her hands were wrinkled, and her eyes,
  Robbed of the girlish light of joy,
Were dim; I felt a sad surprise
  That I had loved her when a boy.

But yet a something in her air
  Restored me to the vanished time;
My heart grew young, and seemed to wear
  The brightness of my youthful prime,
I took her withered hand in mine—
  Its touch recalled a ghost of joy—
I kissed it with a reverent sigh,
  For I had loved her when a boy.

CHARLOTTE PERRY.

THE WIFE'S DESPAIR.

EVADNE.——Act II.—Scene 1.

Evadne. An angel would vainly plead my cause
Within Vicentio's heart—therefore, my lord,
I have no intent to interrupt the rite
That makes that lady yours; but I am come
Thus breathless as you see me—would to heav'n
I could be tearless too!
Hear all the vengeance I intend. I'll tell you.

May you be happy with that happier maid
That never could have loved you more than I do.
But may deserve you better!   May your days,
Like a long stormless summer, glide away,
And peace and trust be with you!
And when at last you close your gentle lives,
Blameless as they were blesséd, may you fall
Into the grave as softly as the leaves
Of two sweet roses on an autumn eve,
Beneath the soft sighs of the western wind;
For myself [*sobbing*] I will but pray
The maker of the lonely beds of peace
To open one of his deep hollow ones,
Where misery goes to sleep, and let me in;
If ever you chance to pass beside my grave,
I am sure you'll not refuse a little sigh,
And if with my friend (I still will call her so),
My friend, Olivia, chide you, pr'ythee tell her
Not to be jealous of me in my grave.

SHEIL.

THE MAID OF THE INN.

Who is she, the poor maniac, whose wildly-fixed eyes
    Seem a heart overcharged to express!
She weeps not, yet often and deeply she sighs;
She never complains, but her silence implies
    The composure of settled distress.

No aid, no compassion the maniac will seek;
    Cold and hunger awake not her care;
Through the rags do the winds of the winter blow
    bleak
On her poor withered bosom, half bare; and her cheek
    Has the deadly pale hue of despair.

Yet cheerful and happy, not distant the day,
　　Poor Mary, the maniac has been;
The traveler remembers, who journeyed this way,
No damsel so lovely, no damsel so gay,
　　As Mary, the maid of the inn.

Her cheerful address filled the guests with delight,
　　As she welcomed them in with a smile;
Her heart was a stranger to childish affright,
And Mary would walk by the abbey at night,
　　When the wind whistled down the dark aisle.

She loved, and young Richard had settled the day,
　　And she hoped to be happy for life;
But Richard was idle and worthless, and they
Who knew her, would pity poor Mary, and say
　　That she was too good for his wife.

'Twas in Autumn, and stormy and dark was the night
　　And fast were the windows and door;
Two guests were enjoying the fire that burnt bright,
And, smoking in silence, with tranquil delight.
　　They listened to hear the wind roar.

" 'Tis pleasant," cried one, " seated by the fireside,
　　To hear the wind whistle without."
"A fine night in the abbey," his comrade replied,
"Methinks a man's courage would now be well tried,
　　Who should wander the ruins about.

" I myself, like a schoolboy, should tremble to hear
　　The hoarse ivy shake over my head;
And could fancy I saw, half persuaded by fear,
Some icy old abbot's white spirit appear,
　　For this wind might awaken the dead."

" I'll wager a dinner," the other one cried,
　　That Mary would venture there now."
" Then wager and lose," with a sneer he replied,

" I'll warrant she'd fancy a ghost by her side,
    And faint if she saw a white cow."

" Will Mary this charge on her courage allow ?"
    His companion exclaimed with a smile ;
" I shall win, for I know she will venture there now,
And earn a new bonnet by bringing a bough
    From the alder that grows in the aisle."

With fearless good humor did Mary comply,
    And her way to the abbey she bent;
The night it was dark, and the wind it was high,
And as hollowly howling it crept through the sky,
    She shivered with cold as she went.

O'er the path, so well known, proceeded the maid,
    Where the abbey rose dim on the sight ;
Through the gateway she entered, she felt not afraid,
Yet the ruins were lonely and wild, and their shade
    Seemed to deepen the gloom of the night.

All around her was silent, save when the rude blast
    Howled dismally round the old pile ;
Over weed-covered fragments still fearless she passed,
And arrived at the innermost ruin at last,
    Where the alder-tree grows in the aisle.

Well pleased did she reach it, and quickly drew near,
    And hastily gathered the bough—
When the sound of a voice seemed to rise on her ear :
She paused, and she listened, all eager to hear,
    And her heart panted fearfully now !

The wind blew, the hoarse ivy shook over her head;—
    She listened ;—naught else could she hear ;
The wind ceased, her heart sank in her bosom with
        dread,
For she heard in the ruins—distinctly—the tread
    Of footsteps approaching her near.

Behind a wide column, half breathless with fear,
    She crept to conceal herself there;
That instant the moon o'er a dark cloud shone clear,
And she saw in the moonlight two ruffians appear,
    And between them—a corpse did they bear!

Then Mary could feel her heart's-blood curdle cold!
    Again the rough wind hurried by—
It blew off the hat of the one, and behold!
Even close to the feet of poor Mary it rolled!—
    She fell—and expected to die!

"Curse the hut!" he exclaims; "Nay come on and first
      hide
    The dead body," his comrade replies—
She beheld them in safety pass on by her side,
She seizes the hat, fear her courage supplied,
    And fast through the abbey she flies.

She ran with wild speed, she rushed in at the door,
    She gazed horribly eager around;
Then her limbs could support their faint burden no
    more,
And exhausted and breathless she sunk on the floor,
    Unable to utter a sound.

Ere yet her pale lips could the story impart,
    For a moment the hat met her view;—
For, Oh God! what cold horror thrilled through her
    heart,
Her eyes from that object convulsively start,
    When the name of her Richard she knew.

Where the old abbey stands, on the common hard by,
    His gibbet is now to be seen;
Not far from the inn it engages the eye,
The traveler beholds it, and thinks, with a sigh,
    Of poor Mary, the maid of the inn.

SOUTHEY.

THE SEASONS.

The Spring-time, O the Spring-time!
  Who does not know it well?
When the little birds begin to build,
  And the buds begin to swell.
When the sun with the clouds plays hide-and-seek,
  And the lambs are bucking and bleating,
And the color mounts to the maiden's cheek,
  And the cuckoo scatters greeting;
    In the Spring-time, joyous Spring-time!

The Summer, O the Summer!
  Who does not know it well?
When the ring-doves coo the long day through,
  And the bee refills his cell.
When the swish of the mower is heard at morn,
  And we all in the woods go roaming,
And waiting is over, and love is born,
  And shy lips meet in the gloaming;
    In the Summer, luscious Summer!

The Autumn, O the Autumn!
  Who does not know it well?
When the leaf turns brown, and the masts drops down,
  And the chestnut splits its shell.
When we muse o'er the days that have gone before,
  And the days that will follow after,
When the grain lies deep on the winnowing-floor,
  And the plump gourd hangs from the rafter;
    In the Autumn, mellow Autumn!

The Winter, O the Winter!
  Who does not know it well?
When, day after day, the fields stretch gray,
  And the peewit wails on the fell.
When we close up the crannies and shut out the cold,
  And the wind sounds hoarse and hollow,
And our dead loves sleep in the churchyard mould,
  And we pray that we soon may follow;
    In the Winter, mournful Winter!

AUSTIN.

THE RELIEF OF LUCKNOW.

Oh, that last day in Lucknow fort!
   We knew that it was the last:
The enemy's lines had crept surely in,
   And the end was coming fast.

To yield to that foe meant worse than death,
   And the men and we all worked on;
It was one day more of smoke and roar,
   And then it would all be done.

There was one of us, a coporal's wife,
   A fair young, gentle thing,
Wasted with fever and with siege,
   And her mind was wandering.

She lay on the ground, in her Scottish plaid,
   And I took her head on my knee;
"When my father comes home frae the pleugh," she
     said,
   "Oh, please then waken me!"

She slept like a child on her father's floor,
   In the flecking of the woodbine shade,
When the house-dog sprawls by the half-open door,
   And the mother's wheel is stayed.

It was smoke and roar and powder stench,
   And hopeless waiting death;
But the soldier's wife, like a full-tired child,
   Seemed scarce to draw her breath.

I sank to sleep, and I had my dream
   Of an English village lane,
And wall and garden, till a sudden scream
   Brought me back to the roar again.

There Jessie Brown stood listening;
   And then a broad gladness broke
All over her face. and she took my hand
   And drew me near, and spoke:

"The Highlanders!   Oh! dinna ye hear
  The slogan far awa'?
The Macgregor's!   Ah! I ken it weel;
  It is the grandest of them a'.

"God bless the bonny Highlanders!
  We're saved! we're saved!" she cried;
And fell on her knees! and thanks to God
  Poured forth like a full flood-tide.

Along the battery line her cry
  Had fallen among the men;
And they started, for they were to die,
  Was life so near them, then?

Then listened for life; and the rattling fire
  Far off, and the far-off roar
Were all; and the colonel shook his head,
  And they turned to their guns once more.

Then Jessie said, "The slogan's dune:
  But can ye no hear them noo?
The Campbells are comin'!   It is nae a dream;
  Our succors hae broken through!"

We heard the roar and rattle afar,
  But the pipers we could not hear;
. So the men plied their work of hopeless war
  And knew that the end was near.

It was not long ere it must be heard,
  A shrilling, ceaseless sound:
It was no noise of the strife afar
  Or the sappers under ground.

It was the pipe of the Highlanders,
  And now they played "Auld Lang Syne;"
It came to our men like the voice of God,
  And they shouted along the line.

And they wept and shook each other's hands,
   And the women sobbed in a crowd,
And every one knelt down where we stood,
   And we all thanked God aloud.

That happy day when we welcomed them in
   Our men put Jessie first;
And the general took her hand, and cheers
   From the men like a volley burst.

And the pipers' ribbons and tartan streamed,
   Marching round and round our line;
And our joyful cheers were broken with tears,
   As the pipers played "Auld Lang Syne."

LOWELL.

OPHELIA'S MAD SCENE.

HAMLET.——Act IV.—Scene 5.

Enter Ophelia, *fantastically dressed, and bedecked with straws and flowers, having gone mad over the death of her old father.*

  Laertes. O, rose of May!
Dear maid, kind sister, sweet Ophelia!—
O Heavens! is't possible, a young maid's wits
Should be as mortal as an old man's life?
Nature is fine in love: and, where 'tis fine,
It sends some precious instance of itself
After the thing it loves.
  Ophelia, sings:
    "They bore him barefaced on the bier;
      Hey non nonny, nonny hey nonny:
    And on his grave rained many a tear;"
Fare you well, my dove!
  Laer. Had'st thou thy wits and didst persuade revenge,
It could not move thus.

Oph. You must sing, "Down a-down, and you call
him a-down-a." O. how the wheel becomes it! It is
the false steward, that stole his master's daughter.

Laer. This nothing's more than matter.

Oph. There's rosemary, that's for remembrance;
pray you, love, remember; and there is pansies, that's
for thoughts.

Laer. A document in madness; thoughts and remembrance fitted.

Oph. There's fennel for you, and columbines; there's
rue for you; and here's some for me:—we may call it
herb of grace o' Sundays:—you may wear your rue
with a difference.—There's a daisy:—I would give you
some violets; but they withered all, when my father
died:—they say he made a good end,—((*sings:*)

"For bonny sweet Robin is all my joy."

Laer. Thought and affliction, passion, hell itself,
She turns to favor and to prettiness.

Oph., (*sings*) "And will he not come again?"
And for all Christian souls! I pray God. God be wi'
you!

SHAKESPEARE.

ONE IN BLUE AND ONE IN GRAY.

Each thin hand resting on a grave
　　Her lips apart in prayer,
A mother knelt and left her tears
　　Upon the violets there.
O'er many a rood of vale and lawn,
　　Of hill and forest gloom,
The reaper Death had revelled in
　　His fearful harvest home.
The last red summer's sun had shown
　　Upon a fruitless fray—
From yonder forest charged the blue,
　　Down yonder slope the grey.

The hush of death was on the scene,
  And sunset o'er the dead,
In that oppressive stillness
  A pall of glory spread.
I know not, dare not question how
  I met the ghastly glare
Of each upturned and stirless face
  That shrunk and whitened there.   ⸱
I knew my noble boys had stood
  Through all that withering day—
I knew that Willie wore the blue,
  That Harry wore the gray.

I thought of Willie's clear blue eye,
  His wavy hair of gold,
That clustered on a fearless brow
  Of purest Saxon mould ;
Of Harry, with his raven locks,
  And eagle glance of pride ;
Of how they clasped each other's hand
  And left their mother's side :
How hand in hand they bore my prayer
  And blessings on the way—
A noble heart beneath the blue,
  Another 'neath the gray.

The dead, with white and folded hands,
  That hushed our village homes,
I've seen laid calmly, tenderly,
  Within their darkened rooms ;
But *there* I saw distorted limbs,
  And many an eye a-glare,
In the soft purple twilight of
  The thunder-smitten air ;
Along the slope and on the sward
  In ghastly ranks they lay,
And there was blood upon the blue,
  And blood upon the gray.

I looked and saw his blood, and his ;
  A swift and vivid dream

Of blended years flashed o'er me, when,
    Like some cold shadow, came
A blindness of the eye and brain—
    The same that seizes one
When men are smitten suddenly
    Who overstare the sun;
And while blurred with the sudden stroke
    That swept my soul, I lay—
They buried Willie in his blue,
    And Harry in his gray.

The shadows fall upon their graves;
    They fall upon my heart;
And through the twilight of my soul
    Like dew the tears will start—
The starlight comes so silently,
    And lingers where they rest;
So hope's revealing starlight sinks
    And shines within my breast.
They ask not there where yonder heaven
    Smiles with eternal day,
Why Willie wore the loyal blue—
    Why Harry wore the gray.

WARD.

——————◆——————

THE FAIR ADVOCATE.

MERCHANT OF VENICE.——Act IV.—Scene 1.

Enter Portia.

Duke. You are welcome: take your place.
Are you acquainted with the difference
That holds this present question in the court?
    Portia. I am informed thoroughly of the cause.
Which is the merchant here, and which the Jew?
    Duke. Antonia and old Shylock, both stand forth

Por. Is your name Shylock?

Shylock. Shylock is my name.

Por. Of a strange nature is the suit you follow;
Yet in such rule, that the Venetian law
Cannot impugn you, as you do proceed—
Then must the Jew be merciful.

Shy. On what compulsion must I? tell me that.

Por. The quality of mercy is not strain'd;
It droppeth, as the gentle rain from heaven,
Upon the place beneath; it is twice bless'd—
It blesseth him that gives, and him that takes;
'Tis mightiest in the mightiest: it becomes
The thronéd monarch better than his crown;
His sceptre shows the force of temporal power,
The attribute to awe and majesty,
Wherein doth sit the dread and fear of kings;
But mercy is above this sceptred sway,
It is enthronéd in the hearts of kings,
It is an attribute to God himself;
And earthly power doth then show likest God's
When mercy seasons justice. Therefore, Jew,
Though justice be thy plea, consider this,—
That in the course of justice, none of us
Should see salvation: we do pray for mercy;
And that same prayer doth teach us all to render
The deeds of mercy. I have spoke thus much
To mitigate the justice of thy plea:
Which if though follow, this strict court of Venice
Must needs give sentence 'gainst the merchant there.

Shy. My deeds upon my head! I crave the law,
The penalty and forfeit of my bond.
We trifle time; I pray thee, pursue sentence.

Por. A pound of that same merchant's flesh is thine;
The court awards it, and the law doth give it.

Shy. Most rightful judge!

Por. And you must cut this flesh from off his breast;
The law allows it and the court awards it.

Shy. Most learned judge;—A sentence; come prepare.

Por. Tarry a little:—there is something else—
This bond doth give thee here no jot of blood;
The words expressly are, a pound of flesh:
Take then thy bond, take thou thy pound of flesh;
But in the cutting of it, if thou dost shed
One drop of Christian blood, thy lands and goods
Are by the laws of Venice, confiscate
Unto the state of Venice.

    Shy. Is that the law?

    Por. Thyself shall see the act:
Why doth the Jew pause? take thy forfeiture.

    Shy. Give me my principal, and let me go.

    Por. He hath refused it in the open court;
He shall have merely justice, and his bond.

    Shy. Shall I not have barely my principal?

    Por. Thou shalt have nothing but the forfeiture,
To be so taken at thy peril, Jew.

    Shy. Why then the devil give him good of it!
I'll stay no longer question.

    Por. Tarry, Jew;
The law hath yet another hold on you.
It is enacted in the laws of Venice,—
If it be proved against an alien,
That by direct or indirect attempts,
He seek the life of any citizen,
The party 'gainst the which he doth contrive,
Shall seize one half his goods: the other half
Comes to the privy coffer of the state;
And the offender's life lies in the mercy
Of the duke only, 'gainst all other voice.
In which predicament I say, thou stand'st.
Down therefore, and beg mercy of the duke.

    Duke. That thou shalt see the difference of our spirit,
I pardon thee thy life, before thou ask it;
For half thy wealth, it is Antonio's;
The other half comes to the general state,
Which humbleness may drive unto a fine.

                   SHAKESPEARE.

THE SLEEP-WALKING SCENE.

MACBETH.——Act V.—Scene 1.

Enter a Doctor *and a* Gentlewoman.

Doctor. I have two nights watched with you. but can perceive no truth in your report. When was it she last walked?

Gentlewoman. Since his majesty went into the field, I have seen her rise from her bed, throw her night-gown upon her, unlock her closet, take forth paper, fold it, write upon it, read it, afterwards seal it, and again return to bed ; yet all this while in a most fast sleep.

Enter Lady Macbeth, *with a taper.*

Lo you, here she comes! This is her very guise ; and upon my life, fast asleep. Observe her; stand close.

Doct. You see, her eyes are open.

Gent. Ay, but their sense is shut.

Doct. What is it she does now? Look, how she rubs her hands.

Gent. It is an accustomed action with her to seem thus washing her hands; I have known her to continue in this a quarter of an hour.

Lady M. Yet here's a spot.

Doct. Hark! she speaks ; I will set down what comes from her, to satisfy my remembrance the more strongly.

Lady M. Out, damned spot! out, I say. One! Two! why then 'tis time to do't:—Hell is murky ;—Fie, my lord, fie, a soldier and afear'd? What need we fear who knows it, when none can call our power to account? Yet who would have thought the old man to have so much blood in him?

Doct. Do you mark that?

Lady M. The thane of Fife had a wife : Where is she now? What, will these hands ne'er be clean? No more o' that, my lord, no more o' that; you mar all with this starting. Here's the smell of the blood still: all the perfumes of Arabia will not sweeten this little hand. Oh! oh! oh!

SHAKESPEARE.

THE PENITENT'S LAMENTATION.

JANE SHORE.——Act V.—Scene 2.

Enter Jane Shore, *her hair hanging loose on her shoulders,
and bare-footed.*

Jane Shore. Yet, yet endure, nor murmur, O my soul!
For are not thy transgressions great and numberless?
Do they not cover thee like rising floods,
And press thee like a weight of waters down?
Wait then with patience, till the circling hours
Shall bring the time of thy appointed rest,
And lay thee down to death.
And hark! methinks the roar of them pursuing,
Sinks like the murmurs of a falling wind,
And softens into silence.   Does revenge
And malice then grow weary and forsake me?
My guards, too, that observ'd me still so close,
Tire in the task of their inhuman office
And loiter far behind.   Alas! I faint,
My spirits fail at once.   The time has been
When this unfriendly door, that bars my passage,
Flew wide, and almost leap'd from off its hinges,
To give me entrance here: when this good house
Has poured forth all its dwellers to receive me;
When my approaches made a little holiday,
And every face was dressed in smiles to meet me;
But now 'tis otherwise; and those who bless'd me,
Now curse me to my face.   Why should I wander,
Stray further on, for I can die ev'n here?
                                        [*She sits down.*
I can no more; [*lies down.*] receive me, thou cold
        earth,
Thou common parent, take me to thy bosom,
And let me rest with thee.
                        Enter Belmour.
· *Belmour.* Upon the ground!
Thy miseries can never lay thee lower.
Look up, thou poor afflicted one! thou mourner,
Whom none has comforted!   Be of courage;—
Your husband lives! 'tis he, my worthiest friend.

Enter Shore.

Jane S. Still art thou there? still dost thou hover
    round me?
Oh, save me, Belmour, from his angry shade!
  Bel. 'Tis he himself! he lives! look up:—
  Jane S. I dare not.
Oh! that my eyes could shut him out for ever.
  Shore. Am I so hateful then, so deadly to thee,
To blast thy eyes with horror? Since I am grown
A burden to the world, myself and thee,
Would I had ne'er survived to see thee more.
  Jane S. Oh! thou most injur'd—dost thou live in-
    deed?
Forgive me!—but forgive me!
  Shore. Be witness for me, ye celestial host,
Such mercy and such pardon as my soul
Accords to thee, and begs of heav'n to show thee,
May such befall me, at my latest hour,
And make my portion blest or curst for ever.
  Jane S. Then all is well, and I shall sleep in peace;—
'Tis very dark, and I have lost you now:—
Was there not something I would have bequeath'd you?
But I have nothing left me to bestow,
Nothing but one sad sigh. O! mercy, heav'n! [*Dies.*

ROWE.

THREE PRAYERS.

Beneath a cross, beyond the town,
  Before a shrine for sorrows made,
Three simple maidens knelt them down,
  And from their hearts devoutly pray'd.
One, dreaming of created things—
  The purple sea, the perfect sky,
Bright, happy birds with painted wings,
  Glad buds that bloom before they die,
The waving woods—the scented air
  Clung to her heart, and through her sighs
Was heard the gentle maiden's pray'r:

"Oh, give me beauty for my prize!"
A hidden furnace seemed to glow
Within the second maiden's breast.
She heard the stirring trumpet blow,
  She saw the warrior's plume and crest;
Ambition dazzled in her eyes
  That life's reward—a deathless name,
Then from her heart came stifled cries:
  "If I may live, oh! give me fame."
The third fair maiden knelt apart;
  Her eyes—a heaven starr'd with tears,
Her white arms folded on her heart,
  She faced a mystery of years.
A sudden rapture seemed to lift
  Her very soul to heav'n above:
"Be mine," she pray'd, "this priceless gift:
"Let me be loved by one I love!"

CLEMENT SCOTT.

A QUEEN'S DEFENCE.
WINTER'S TALE.——Act III.—Scene 2.

Officer; "Hermione, queen to the worthy Leontes, king of Sicilia, thou art here accused and arraigned of high treason, in committing adultery with Polixenes, king of Bohemia; and conspiring with Camillo to take away the life of our sovereign lord the king, thy royal husband; the pretence whereof being by circumstances partly laid open, thou, Hermione, contrary to the faith and allegiance of a true subject, didst counsel and aid them, for their better safety, to fly away by night."

Hermione. Since what I am to say, must be but that
Which contradicts my accusation; and
The testimony on my part, no other
But what comes from myself: it shall scarce boot me
To say, *Not guilty;* mine integrity

Being counted falsehood, shall, as I express it,
Be so received.   But thus,—If powers divine
Behold our human actions as they do,
I doubt not then, but innocence shall make
False accusation blush, and tyranny
Tremble at patience.—You, my lord, best know
(Who least will seem to do so) my past life
Hath been as continent, as chaste, as true,
As I am now unhappy; which is more
Than history can pattern, though devised,
And play'd, to take spectators: For behold me,
A moiety of the king, a great king's daughter,
The mother to a hopeful prince,—here standing,
To prate and talk for life, and honor, 'fore
Who please to come and hear.   For life, I prize it
As I weigh grief, which I would spare: for honor,
'Tis a derivative from me to mine,
And only that I stand for.   I appeal
To your own conscience, sir, before Polixenes
Came to your court, how I was in your grace,
How merited to be so; since he came,
With what encounter so uncurrent I
Have strain'd to appear thus : if one jot beyond
The bound of honor, or in act or will
That way inclining, harden'd be the hearts
Of all that hear me, and my near'st of kin
Cry, Fie upon my grave!

SHAKESPEARE.

SOMEBODY'S MOTHER.

The woman was old, and ragged and gray,
And bent with the chill of a winter's day;
The streets were white with a recent snow,
And the woman's feet with age were slow.

At the crowded crossing she waited long,
Jostled aside by the careless throng
Of human beings who passed her by,
Unheeding the glance of her anxious eye.

Down the street with laughter and shout,
Glad in the freedom of "school is out,"
Came happy boys, like a flock of sheep,
Hailing the snow piled white and deep;
Past the woman, so old and gray,
Hasten the children on their way.

None offered a helping hand to her,
So weak and timid, afraid to stir,
Lest the carriage wheels or the horses' feet
Should trample her down in the slippery street.

At last came out of the merry troop
The gayest boy of all the group;
He paused beside her, and whispered low,
"I'll help you across, if you wish to go."

Her aged hand on his strong young arm
She placed, and so without hurt or harm,
He guided the trembling feet along,
Proud that his own were young and strong;
Then back again to his friends he went,
His young heart happy and well content.

"She's somebody's mother, boys, you know,
For all she's aged, and poor and slow;
And some one, some time, may lend a hand
To help my mother—you understand?—
If ever she's poor, and old and grey,
And her own dear boy so far away."

"Somebody's mother bowed low her head,
In her home that night, and the prayer she said
Was: "God be kind to that noble boy,
Who is somebody's son and pride and joy."

Faint was the voice, and worn and weak,
But heaven lists when its chosen speak;
Angels caught the faltering word,
And "Somebody's Mother's" prayer was heard.

MARY D. BRINE.

CHRISTMAS MEMORIES.

The Christmas bells across the snow
    Are ringing out good-will to men;
Away the merry skaters go
    Across the fields, along the fen ;
God's wind of peace and love has blown
    The clouds from sorrow-stricken skies :
Yet, I am sitting here alone
    With my old Christmas Memories !

Cease Christmas chime ! that wildly rings
    The knell of man's delayed desire !
She at the piano touch'd the strings,
    Whilst I sat dreaming by the fire.
'Tis mystical when souls entwine,
    When sympathetic longings blend—
She came, and placed her hand in mine,
    And then she whispered, " Be my friend ! "

Who could that longing look resist !
    The blue of those Madonna eyes ;
The hair—the parted lips unkist ;
    The depth of all her broken sighs ?
I took her hand—nor seemed to trace
    A storm on such a summer sea.
Oh, God ! I see her haunting face
    That pleaded, " Be a friend to me ! "

One night the books were cast aside,
    The poem hush'd that I had read,
We only heard the wind outside,
    The firelight touch'd her golden head.
We were alone ! none other ! none !
    Have mercy on me, God above !
She weeping, said : " What have you done ?
    This is not friendship ; it is love ! "

Yes : it was love, untamed and wild
    That through our hearts and pulses ran,
The first affection of a child,

The last great passion of a man!
No love like this was ever born
    To touch my tears, to cloud my sight;
She was my waking thought at morn,
    She was my parting prayer at night.

Yes! it was love, so pure, that I
    Can feel it dim my eyelids yet:
It made our spring a memory,
    Our summer one profound regret;
We only met to love the more
    Beneath the blossom-covered tree,
We loved in silence on the shore,
    And speechless, looking out to sea!

Cold Christmas chimes! why ceaseless ring,
    Across the snow, your endless knell ;
It whispers of remembered spring
    And tolls for our supreme farewell?
Oh! wingéd love! for love is wild
    And has been since the world began,
It bears away the loving child
    And leaves alone the thinking man!

So, merry skaters, hand in hand,
    Laugh on until the sun has set ;
Together you will find love's land,
    Then dream together—and forget.
Away! you lovers! off you go
    Across the fields, along the fen ;
For Christmas bells, above the snow,
    Are ringing out good will to men!

—L' Envoi!—

But when you see old friends depart
    And find that love is sweet—but dies ;
Pray God that all your life and heart
    Be free from Christmas memories!

CLEMENT SCOTT.

THE DEATH OF EGYPT'S QUEEN.

ANTONY AND CLEOPATRA.——Act V.—Scene 2.

Cleopatra. Give me my robe, put on my crown; I
    have Immortal longings in me: Now no more
The juice of Egypt's grape shall moist this lip:—
Yare, yare, good Iras; quick.—Methinks I hear
Antony call; I see him rouse himself
To praise my noble act; I hear him mock
The luck of Cæsar, which the gods give men
To excuse their after wrath : Husband, I come:
Now to that name my courage prove my title !
I am fire and air ; my other elements
I give to baser life.—So,—have you done?
Come, then, and take the last warmth of my lips.
Farewell, kind Charmian!—Iras, long farewell!
[*Kisses her maids,* Charmian *and* Iras—*the latter falls
             and dies.*
Have I the aspick in my lips?   Dost fall?
If thou and nature can so gently part,
The stroke of death is as a lover's pinch,
Which hurts, and is desired.   Dost thou lie still?
If thus thou vanishest, thou tell'st the world
It is not worth leave-taking.   [may say,
  Charmian. Dissolve, thick cloud and rain; that I
The gods themselves do weep !
  Cleo. This proves me base :
If she first meet the curled Antony,
He'll make demand of her : and spend that kiss
Which is my heaven to have.   Come, mortal wretch,
        [*To the asp, which she applies to her breast.*
With thy sharp teeth this knot intrinsicate
Of life at once untie, poor venomous fool,
Be angry and despatch.   O, couldst thou speak !
That I might hear thee call great Cæsar, ass
Unpolicied !
  Char. O eastern star !   *Cleo.* Peace, peace !
Dost thou not see my baby at my breast,
That sucks the nurse asleep ?

Char. O, break! O, break!
Cleo. As sweet as balm, as soft as air, as gentle,—
O Antony!—Nay, I will take thee too : [*Applying another asp.*
What should I stay—   [*Falls on a bed and dies.*

                                        SHAKESPEARE.

"PERSEVERE."

Robert, the Bruce, in the dungeon stood
    Waiting the hour of doom :
Behind him the Palace of Holyrood,
    Before him, a nameless tomb,
And the foam on his lip was flecked with red,
    As away to the past his memory sped,
Upcalling the day of his great renown
    When he won and he wore the Scottish crown;
Yet come there shadow, or come there shine,
    The spider is spinning his thread so fine.
" I have sat on the royal seat of Scone,"
    He muttered below his breath;
"It's a luckless change, from a kingly throne
    To a felon's shameful death."
And he clenched his hand in his despair,
    And he struck at the shapes that were gathered there
Pacing his cell in impatient rage,
    As a new-caught lion paces his cage ;
But come there shadow or come there shine.
    The spider is spinning his web so fine.
" Oh, were it my fate to yield up my life
    At the head of my liegemen all,
In the foremost shock of the battle-strife
    Breaking my country's thrall,
I'd welcome death from the foeman's steel,
    Breathing a prayer for old Scotland's weal ;
But here, where no pitying heart is nigh,
    By a loathsome hand it is hard to die;
Yet come there shadow, or come there shine,
    The spider is spinning his thread so fine.
" Time and again have I fronted the pride

Of the tyrant's vast array,
But only to see, on the crimson tide,
My hopes swept far away.
Now a landless chief, and a crownless king,
On the broad, broad earth, not a living thing
To keep me court, save yon insect small
Striving to reach from wall to wall:"
For come there shadow, or come there shine,
The spider is spinning his thread so fine.

"Work—work as a fool, as I have done,
To the loss of your time and pain—
The space is too wide to be bridged across,
You but waste your strength in vain."
And Bruce, for the moment, forgot his grief,
His soul now filled with the same belief,
That howsoever the issue went,
For evil or good was the omen sent;
And come there shadow, etc.

As a gambler watches his turning card
On which his all is staked;
As a mother waits for the hopeful word
For which her soul has ached;
It was thus Bruce watch'd with every sense
Centered alone in that look intense;
All rigid he stood with unuttered breath,
Now white, now red, but still as death;
Yet come there shadow, or come there shine,
The spider is spinning his thread so fine.

Six several times the creature tried,
When at the seventh; "See—see!
He has spanned it over," the captive cried,
"Lo! a bridge of hope to me;
Thee, God, I thank—for this lesson here
Has tutored my soul to Persevere!"
And it served him well, for ere long he wore
In freedom the Scottish crown once more;
And come there shadow, or come there shine,
The spider is spinning his thread so fine.

BROUGHAM.

FATHER AND DAUGHTER.

King Lear *asleep on a couch,* Cordelia, *seated,* Physician *and* •
two Knights standing by him.

Cordelia. All blessed secrets;
All you unpublished virtues of the earth,
Spring with my tears—be aidant and remediate,
In the good man's distress—
Oh, you kind heavens,
Cure this great breach in his abused nature;
Th' untuned and jarring senses, oh, wind up,
Of this child changed father.   [art,
Physician. We have employed the utmost pow'r of
And this deep rest will perfect our design.
Cor. Oh, Regan! Goneril! Inhuman sisters!
Had he not been your father, these white hairs
Had challenged, sure some, pity ! Was this a face
To be exposed against the warring winds?
My enemy's dog, though he had bit me, should
Have stood that night against my fire.
Phys. Be by, good madam, when we do awake him;
I doubt not of his temperance.
Cor. Is he arrayed?
Phys.. Ay, madam, in the heaviness of his sleep
We put fresh garments on him.
Cor. Oh, my dear father! Restoration, hang
Thy med'cine on my lips; and let this kiss
Repair those violent harms, that my two sisters
Have in thy rev'rence made. He wakes.
                                    [Lear *is seated*
Speak to him.
Phys. Madam, do you; 'tis fittest.   [jesty ?
Cor. How does my royal lord? How fares your ma-
Lear. You do me wrong to take me out o' th' grave.
Lear *rises, and* Cordelia *supports him down to the front of*
the Stage.
Cor. Speak to me, sir; who am I?
Lear. You are a soul in bliss; but I am bound
Upon a wheel of fire, which my own tears
Do scald like molten lead.

Cor. Sir, do you know me?

Lear. You are a spirit, I know; when did you die?

Cor. Still, still far wide.　　　　　　[*more composed.*

Phys. Madam, he's scarce awake; he'll soon grow

Lear. Where have I been? Where am I? Fair day-
　　light?
I am mightily abused: I should even die with pity
To see another thus.　I will not swear
These are my hands.

Cor. Oh, look upon me, sir,
And hold your hand in blessing o'er me.　(Lear *at-
　　tempts to kneel,*)—Nay,
You must not kneel.

Lear. Pray, do not mock me:
I am a very foolish, fond old man,
Fourscore and upward; and, to deal plainly,
I fear I am not in my perfect mind.　　　　　[*me*

Cor. Nay, then, farewell to patience!　Witness for
Ye mighty pow'rs, I n'er complained till now!

Lear. Methinks, I should know you, and know this
　　man;
Yet I am doubtful; for I'm mainly ignorant
What place this is; and all the skill I have
Remembers not these garments; nor do I know
Where I did sleep last night—Pray, do not mock me;
For, as I am a man, I think that lady
To be my child Cordelia.

Cor. Oh, my dear, dear father!　　　　　[*weep.*

Lear. Be your tears wet?　Yes, faith: pray, do not
I know I have given thee cause, and am so humbled
With crosses since, that I could ask
Forgiveness of thee, were it possible
That thou couldst grant it;
If thou hast poison for me, I will drink it,
Bless thee, and die,

Cor. Oh, pity, sir, a bleeding heart, and cease
This killing language.

Lear. Tell me, friends, where am I?

Phys. In your own kingdom, sir,

Lear. Do not abuse me,

Phys. Be comforted, good madam, for the violence
Of his distemper's past: we'll lead him in,
Nor trouble him, till he's better settled.
Will it please you, sir, walk into freer air?
    Lear. You must bear with me, I am old and foolish;
Forget and forgive.

Physician *leads off* King Lear,

    Cor. The gods restore you,   [*a distant march.*
Hark, I hear afar
The beaten drum.   Old Kent's a man of's word.
Oh! for an arm
Like the fierce thunderer's, when the earth-born sons
Stormed heaven, to fight this injured father's battle;
That I could shift my sex, and dye me deep
In his opposer's blood!   But as I may,
With women's weapons, piety and pray'rs,
I'll aid his cause.—You never-erring gods,
Fight on his side, and thunder on his foes
Such tempests, as his poor aged head sustained!
Your image suffers when a monarch bleeds;
'Tis your own cause; for that your succors bring;
Revenge yourselves, and right an injured king.

SHAKESPEARE.

THE TELEGRAPH CLERK.

With aching eyes and fingers worn
    By private craze and public crash,
I sit and slave from night to morn,
    And do my turn at "dot" and "dash."
I see that some are free to roam,
    To rest a little while and laugh ;
But this small office is my home,
    Where I've to work the Telegraph.

The messages come pouring in—
    From ALICE "love ;" a growl from DICK ;
I know what horse is bound to win ;

But still this everlasting click!
At home, my dear, I cannot dine,"
Wires craftily some better half;
Would his reversion could be mine,
But I've to work the Telegraph;
My fingers spin the ball that whirls
The world's roulette from dawn to dark;
I plead for broken-hearted girls,
And catch the unsuspecting clerk;
I'm messenger of life and death,
The voice of fate, the jester's chaff;
'Tis mine—the universal breath—
Whilst I command the Telegraph!

Within my breast securely locked,
I hold the secrets of the town;
Life hangs on me when lines are blocked,
Without me commerce tumbles down.
The great world stops when work is done;
There's rest for managers and staff,
But for the operator—none;
He still must work the Telegraph!

In summer time I scent the breeze
That comes from mountain and from sea,
I seem to hear the waving trees
Conveyed by Electricity;
I "touch" the towns where maidens skate,
And long, these winter days, to laugh;
Why moan? when I manipulate
The Departmental Telegraph!

O, fellow-workers! we but ask—
Not as a favor but a right.
Some slight concession in our task,
A pause by day, some rest at night.
We ask for bread, and not a stone—
The whole of prospect, not the half.
Come! earn the blessing, not the groan,
Of men who work the Telegraph!

CLEMENT SCOTT.

THE ROYAL WIDOW WOOED.

RICHARD III.——Act II.—Scene 1.

Lady Anne. Hung be the heavens with black; yield
    day to night:
Comets importing change of times and states,
Brandish your fiery tresses in the sky,
And with them scourge the bad revolting stars,
That have consented to King Henry's death.
Oh! be accurst the hand that had shed his blood,
Accurst the head that had the heart to do it!
If ever he have a wife, let her be made
More miserable by the life of him,
Than I am now, by Edward's death and thine!
    Gloster. Poor girl, what pains she takes to curse
    herself. (*Aside.*)
    Lady A. If ever he have a child, abortive be it,
Prodigious, and untimely brought to light,
Whose hideous form, whose most unnatural aspect
May fright the hopeful mother at her view,
And that be heir to his unhappiness!
Now on to Chertsey with your sacred load.
    Glos. (*Advancing.*) Stay, you that bear the corse,
    and set it down,
       *   *   *   *   *   * [fiend?
    Lady A. Why dost thou haunt him thus, unsated
Thou hast but power over his mortal body;
His soul thou canst not reach, therefore be gone.
    Glos. Sweet saint, be not so hard, for charity.
    Lady A. If thou delight to view thy heinous deeds,
Behold this pattern of thy butcheries.
Why didst thou do this deed?   Could not the laws
Of man, of nature, nor of heav'n dissuade thee?
No beast so fierce, but knows some touch of pity.
    Glos. If want of pity be a crime so hateful,
How comes it thou, fair excellence, art guilty?
    Lady A. What means the slanderer?
    Glos. Vouchsafe, divine perfection of a woman,
Of these my crimes supposed, to give me leave
By circumstance but to acquit myself.

*   *   *   *   *   *

Lady A. Thou wert the cause, and most accurst
    effect.

Glos. Your beauty was the cause of that effect:
Your beauty, that did haunt me in my sleep
To undertake the death of all the world,
So I might live one hour in that soft bosom!

Lady A. If I thought that, I tell thee, homicide,
These hands should rend that beauty from my cheeks.

Glos. These eyes could not endure that beauty's
    wreck:
You should not blemish it, if I stood by:
As all the world is nourished by the sun,
So I by that: it is my day, my life!

Lady A. I would it were, to be revenged on thee.

Glos. It is a quarrel most unnatural,
To wish revenge on him that loves thee.

Lady A. Say, rather, 'tis my duty,
To seek revenge on him that killed my husband.

Glos. Fair creature, he that killed thy husband,
Did it to help thee to a better husband.

 Lady A. His better does not breathe upon the earth.

*   *   *   *   *   *

Glos. (*Rises.*) Then bid me kill myself, and I will
    do it

Lady A. I have already.

Glos. That was in thy rage;
Say it again, and even with thy word,
This guilty hand, that robbed thee of thy love,
Shall, for thy love, revenge thee on thy lover;
To both their deaths shalt thou be accessary.

Glos. What, not a word, to pardon or condemn me;
But thou art wise—and canst with silence kill me;
Yet, even in death, my fleeting soul pursues thee:—
Dash not the tears of penitence away!

Lady A. Would'st thou not blame me to forgive thy
    crimes?

Glos. They are not to be forgiven; no, not even
Penitence can atone them!—Oh, misery
Of thought—that strikes me with at once repentance
And despair!—Though unpardoned, yield me pity!

Lady A. Would I knew thy heart!
Glos. 'Tis figured in my tongue.
Lady A. I fear me, both are false.
Glos. Then never man was true!
Lady A. Put up thy sword.
Glos. Say, then, my peace is made.
Lady A. That shalt thou know hereafter.
Glos. But shall I live in hope?
Lady A. All men, I hope, live so.
Glos. Vouchsafe to wear this ring.
Lady A. To take is not to give.
Glos. See how the ring encompasseth thy finger,
Even so thy breast encloseth my poor heart;
Wear both of them, for both of them are thine.
I swear, bright saint, I am not what I was.
Those eyes have turned these stubborn heart to woman;
Thy goodness makes me soft in penitence,
And my harsh thoughts are turned to peace and love.
Oh! if thy poor devoted servant might
But beg one favor at thy gracious hand,
Thou wouldst confirm his happiness forever.
  Lady A. What is it?   [signs
  Glos. That it may please thee, leave these sad de-
To him that has most cause to be a mourner
And presently repair to Crosby house,
Where—after I have solemnly interred
At Chertsey monast'ry this injured king,
And wet his grave with my repentant tears,
I will with all expedient duty see you.
For divers unknown reasons, I beseech you,
Grant me this favor.
  Lady A. I do, my lord—and much it joys me, too,
To see you are become so penitent!—

                                    SHAKESPEARE.

                    THE END.

www.ingramcontent.com/pod-product-compliance
Lightning Source LLC
Chambersburg PA
CBHW032012010726
47493CB00007B/2360